Patty June 1971

GOOD OLD
ARCHIBALD

Good Old Archibald

by

Ethelyn M. Parkinson

Illustrated by Mary Stevens

New York   **ABINGDON PRESS**   Nashville

TO GERALD, KEITH, AND LOUISE
their sister dedicates this book
in memory of the happy days

Contents

CHAPTER I

Good Old Ralph

In Brookfield School, things happen fast, sometimes. So, before anything else happens, I, Trenton J. Conway, Junior, am going to write down some important events of the past four weeks, just for the records.

First, good old Ralph Jackson moved away and left his seat and desk in Miss Kramer's room very empty.

The Monday morning after that, the guys stood around in the schoolyard eating their salted peanuts very sadly.

Wilmer Pitkin looked saddest because Wilmer had a black eye, and there is something very sad about one black eye and one blue one.

"Good old Ralph!" Wilmer said. "He is gone, but not forgotten. I miss him. I feel bad. I do not feel like playing baseball, and the big game is only four weeks away. Maybe the Lawson Lions will beat us Brookfield Bumble-bees this year."

The Bumblebees always play the Lawson Lions on picnic day, and our mothers always come to watch. Ralph had been a very good player.

"Yes, this is hard to take," Wilmer said. He licked some salt off his fingers and wiped his fingers on his pants. He said, "Any more peanuts, Harley? I need a few more to brace me up."

"Take some," said Harley Scott. "Wait." Harley took a few first.

Harley has black hair; and as soon as he is eighteen, he is going to join the Marines and have a black mustache to scare the girls away.

But Harley has feelings. He said, "I am going to miss Ralph when we sing 'The Marines' Hymn.' Won't you miss good old Ralph when we sing 'The Marines' Hymn,' Trent?"

Now even though it is true that I am the captain of the Bumblebees, I am just a plain guy with a butch cut and freckles and a loud voice. But under my sweater I am not just skin and knobby bones. I have feelings, too, and I felt sad.

I swallowed my last peanut. "One more peanut, Harley," I said. "Yes, Ralph sang it loud."

"And all on one note," added Wonderful Wanda Wilson.

Wanda was standing behind me, with Gorgeous Glenora Jones and Harley's cousin, Susie Scott. They are always listening in.

"What about you, Wanda?" Harley said. "I will now sing a little to show how you sound." Harley opened his mouth wide, shut his eyes, and sang: "Sa-ha-hanta Loo-hoo-cheeya! San-taw Loo-chee-yaw!"

"Very funny!" Wanda said. She shook back her pony tails.

Wanda has two yellow pony tails and eyes that are the color of my blue china piggy bank.

She said, "I sing the tune, don't I, Trent?"

"I will answer that," Wilmer said. Wilmer is a very great thinker. He always knows what to say. "No one would ever get lonesome for your singing, Wanda," he said. "You flitter around too much from high to low. Ralph did not flitter around. Ralph always sang C-sharp, and you could depend on it. Right, Harley?"

"Right!" Harley said. "Ralph sang C-sharp in kindergarten, and kept right on. When good old Ralph is one hundred, he will still sing C-sharp."

"Loud!" said Glenora. She put her hands over her ears, flopped her funny black eyelashes at Harley, and laughed. "I can hear him now!"

Susie giggled. "I hear a horrible sound, too. But it isn't Ralph. It's the bell."

It was the first bell, and I said, "I hate to go in and look at good old Ralph's empty seat and desk."

11

"So do I," Wilmer said. "Ralph even took his horse chestnut."

Just then something happened. A very long, shiny car stopped in front of the school, and a boy got out of it. He stood there on the walk and looked at us, and we looked at him.

"Who is that?" Wilmer said. "He does not look like any guy I ever saw."

The boy was dressed up in a gray jacket, gray pants, a white shirt, and a necktie. He had a wrist watch and a ring. His hair looked kind of red and kind of brown, and it was combed down very slick.

"Well," I said, "my mother says you should not look at other people's clothes. Inside his best clothes, he is just a guy, maybe."

"He can't play ball in his best clothes," Wilmer said. "Victor Valley would laugh him out of town."

Victor Valley is captain of the Lawson Lions. He is thirteen and a very hard man.

The girls had their arms around each other, and they were smiling at the strange boy.

"Oh, isn't he keen?" Wanda said. Her eyes were very round. "Oh, isn't he neat? Tee-hee! I hope he's in our room!"

"Maybe he is in our room," Susie said. "He's just as tall as Trent and Harley and Wilmer. Tee-hee! I hope he's in our room."

"So do I," Glenora said. She poked Wanda, and then

she ran, and Wanda chased her. They ran in a circle around us laughing. "Oh! Hee-hee! Hee-hee!"

Susie jumped up high in her blue plaid skirt, and the flowers fell off her pony tail.

"Well," I said, "look at some people wasting giggles and high jumps."

Wilmer said, "I-hope-he's-in-our-room-I-hope-he's-in-our-room-I-hope-he's-in-our-room!"

Harley said, "It is easy to see that some people are not sad because good old Ralph is gone-but-not-forgotten. They will be very happy to see the Lawson Lions win the big game and be the champions!"

The second bell rang, and we ran in. Susie stopped on the stairs to fix her flowers, and the new boy caught up with her.

"Good morning," he said. "I am Archibald Brewster. I shall be attending your school. Where is the principal's office, please?"

"Hce-hee, it's right there!" Susie said. She pointed at Miss Buckmaster, standing in her door. "Hee-hee!" she said again.

"Thank you," Archibald said. He walked over to Miss Buckmaster, and the rest of us went into Miss Kramer's room.

But in a minute there was a tap on the door. Miss Kramer went into the hall, and we could hear Miss Buckmaster's voice. Then Miss Kramer brought Archibald into our room.

"Boys and girls," she said, "you will all be very happy to know that we have a new boy in our class. His name is Archibald Brewster, and he will have Ralph Jackson's seat."

Well, it did not make us happy to see someone else in good old Ralph's seat, putting his books in good old Ralph's desk.

"We are going to sing this morning," Miss Kramer said. "Who has a choice?"

The fellows raised their hands.

"Harley," she said, "what do you wish to sing—as if I didn't know?"

" 'The Marines' Hymn,' " Harley said.

"The Marines' Hymn" sounded very strange without Ralph's good old C-sharp. It was very sad to see Archibald Brewster sitting there tapping on Ralph's desk with one finger but not singing.

He was as smart as Wonderful Wanda. He got one hundred in arithmetic and one hundred in spelling. But we boys knew he was just showing off.

At recess he stayed in Ralph's seat to pile his books neatly in the desk. We walked over and watched him.

"Well," Harley said, "Ralph is gone."

"Yes, Ralph is gone," Wilmer said. "We have nothing to remember him by."

"Right!" said Susie. "A black eye can't last forever, Wilmer Pitkin, but I think the one Ralph gave you will last another week."

"Very funny!" Wilmer said. "It was all a mistake."

"Yes!" I said. "Two mistakes. Pitkin made them both. First, he struck Ralph out, and then he couldn't run away fast enough. Good old Ralph was the fastest Bumblebee. He could really run!"

"And hit!" Wanda said. "And it is very impolite to talk over Archibald's head this way."

"Oh, I don't mind," Archibald said. "In fact, if you wish to put a few flowers on this desk in memory of Ralph, I shall be very careful not to spill the water."

This was a very queer speech. We did not know any other guy who would make a speech like that.

But then, we did not know any other guy who had a real gold wrist watch or a ring with a brown stone in it.

We did not know any other guy who wore his best gray jacket to school with a white shirt and necktie, or who put smelly stuff on his hair to plaster down the curls.

I sniffed. "What do I smell?" I said. "It smells like the dear little flowers in spring."

Wanda sniffed, too. "I smell that big chew of terrible mint gum in your pocket, Trent Conway!" she said. "When you chew that, everyone will think you have mumps."

"I will not chew all of it," I said. "I am gum banker for the guys this week."

All the girls tried to turn pale. But it was only a joke, and all the guys laughed except Archibald. He looked very worried.

"Boys and girls," Miss Kramer said, "you are missing some nice sunshine."

So we went out to play.

"Well," Harley said, "I feel too sad to play baseball, but good old Ralph would wish us to bat a little."

"Yes," I said. "Ralph is gone-but-not-forgotten, but life has to go on. First batter!"

Archibald was standing there waiting.

We did not want to bother with Archibald, but the Brookfield Bumblebees are very polite.

"A-hem!" I said. "Archibald, you can be outfielder. If you have to scramble through the hedge and get the ball, be careful on the other side. That's where Mr. Walton keeps his mad dog."

Archibald put his hands in his pockets. "I should like to observe the game this morning," he said.

Observe.

Harley said, "You can't sing 'The Marines' Hymn'! Can't you even play baseball?"

"I have played indoor softball," Archibald said. "Tennis is my outdoor game."

Tennis.

Wilmer said, "In Brookfield only girls play tennis. There is only one tennis court in this town, and big girls always have it."

"One court?" Archibald said. "Why is that?"

I explained. "My dad says this town needs more industry. Brookfield needs to grow. Then there will be more money for schools and parks and things."

"Perhaps I'll have a tennis court of my own," Archibald said.

"In Ralph's back yard?" said Harley.

"I didn't move into good old Ralph's house," Archibald said. "I'm living in a white house on Maxwell Street, at present."

At present.

There is only one white house on Maxwell Street. Wilmer's eyes popped, although the black one could not pop much.

Wilmer said, "You mean the big, empty house with a fence around it?"

"Yes," Archibald said. "It belongs to my father's Aunt

17

Grace. She has come to live there for a while. There is a very large back lawn. Baker will make me a tennis court if I ask him."

We all stood in a circle around Archibald.

"Baker? Who's Baker?" I asked.

"Why, Baker is the man."

"Do you mean he's your dad?"

"Oh, no!" Archibald said. "My father is too busy to bother. And he's too far away. Baker drives the car."

Harley said, "You mean you hire a man just to drive?"

"Baker does other things, of course," Archibald said. "He mows the lawn. Who mows your lawn, Trent?"

"I do," I said, "if Ma can catch me. Or one of my brothers, if Ma can catch one."

Archibald stared. "Have you *two* brothers, Trent?"

"Two? Ha!" I said. "I have six." I pointed around the schoolyard. "There's Shannon, with the red hair. That's one. He's in Fifth, and he's the best cook next to Ma. The Third Grader who just batted a home run is Hanky. He's one. The pitcher is Kymie. He's in Third, too, and he's one. Then there're Joel and Jerry, those twins, yelling loudest in the marble game. They're in Second. And Corky's around on the kindergarten side. He looks like me, with light brown hair and freckles. He's one. There's one almost anywhere you look. Who lives at your house, Archibald?"

"Well," Archibald said, "there's Father's Aunt Grace. That's one. And I."

18

"That's two," I said. "Go on."

"Well, there's the help. That's all at present. My mother has tuberculosis, and she has to stay in a sanitarium until she's well."

"Too bad," Harley said. "Any brothers?"

Archibald shook his head. "I have a dog."

A dog. All the guys have dogs. We all turned back to the game.

"Come on," Wilmer said. "Let's play ball!"

"O.K.! No women on the field!" I yelled. "First batter up!"

Archibald sat on the walk with his hands in his pockets, and watched.

Wilmer Pitkin wound up and sent one ball at me. "Strike one!" he yelled.

"That was a ball, and you know it, Pitkin!" I said.

"Strike one!" he yelled again.

I threw down the bat. "It was a ball, and if you don't know it, I'll teach you!" I said.

But the bell rang.

"We will not waste another recess on Archibald," Wilmer said. "I have just had a terrible thought. If we are friendly, he will want to play. And if he is on the team, we will lose the big game for sure. So watch it, men, watch it!"

19

CHAPTER II

Plight of the Bumblebees

After school we started home down Oak Street, and Archibald Brewster tried to walk with us.

"You don't live this way, Archibald," Wilmer Pitkin said.

"You live over on Maxwell," said Harley Scott.

I said, "If you walk down Oak Street, you will just have to walk back."

"No, I won't," Archibald said. "Don't you see that big car coming behind us? That's Baker. My Aunt Grace has sent him. Whenever I'm ready, he will drive me home. I am not ready, yet. Where is your house, Trent?"

I moaned. I was afraid of this. Archibald was coming to see me! I did not want to bother with a boy like Archibald. And we did not want him on the Bumblebees team.

But before I knew it, we were standing in front of my house. "Well, this is it," I said.

My house is square and white. There is a long porch across the front of it. There is a side porch, and there is a back porch.

Archibald looked at my house a long time. He said, "Do you sleep upstairs, Trent?"

I said, "We all sleep upstairs, except Pa and Ma."

"Show me your window," Archibald said.

I pointed to a front window over the porch. "That's my room and Shannon's," I said. "The one next to it belongs to Hanky and Kymie. They are painting a Diesel on the wall. The room just back of mine belongs to Joel and Jerry. Corky just visits around."

"The twins don't have a good view," Archibald said. "They can't see the street."

"Oh, but they have the clothes chute," Wilmer said. "Nobody else has the clothes chute."

Archibald was staring at the side of the house. "Say, Trent!" he said. "Do you see something that looks like a coffee can clattering down the side of your house?"

"Yes," I said. "That's the Lightning Express. Hanky and Kymie are sending down for cookies. Watch!"

The Lightning Express is a coffee can on a rope. Hanky and Kymie send it out the hall window down to the kitchen. Ma puts cookies in it, and they pull it up.

They were hanging way out the window now. They

are skinny guys. Hank's hair is black, and Kymie's is red like Shannon's. They are the same age because one of them is adopted.

The kitchen window screen pushed out, and we saw Ma's hand reaching. The can disappeared. In a minute it was on the window sill again and the screen closed.

"Watch me flag down the Express!" I said. I took five leaps toward the kitchen window and reached for the can, but it was dangling just above my hand. Kymie howled for Ma.

I went back to the sidewalk. Wilmer and Harley were doubled up laughing. Archibald looked very worried.

I slapped my hands together. "Well, that's that!" I said. "No cookies!"

"I didn't want any," Archibald said. "Where is your doghouse?"

"Doghouse?" I said. "What doghouse?"

"You said you had a dog."

"I didn't say we had a doghouse. Toby just visits around like Corky."

"Our dog has a doghouse," Archibald said.

I said, "What's good enough for us is good enough for Toby."

Just then the side door opened, and my dad came out on the porch in an apron. He had a pair of shears in one hand, and he put the other hand up to his mouth.

"Hear ye! Hear ye!" he yelled. "The Trenton J. Conway, Senior, Barber Shop is now open for business. Free

22

haircuts to the first ten customers! A dollar for every shave!"

Wilmer giggled. "Look out for your big, black mustache, Harley!" he whispered.

Archibald stepped back a little. "Who is that man?" he said.

"It's Pa," I told him.

"Is he a barber?"

"In office hours he is a poor, worried lawyer," I said. "But around home he cuts everyone's hair twice a month." I wiggled over a little so Pa could not see me.

"Hear ye! Hear ye!" Pa yelled. "Free haircuts on me, and if there isn't some business here in five seconds, I'm coming after some!"

Two things happened. Mr. Miller, our next door neighbor, opened his door and yelled, "Be right there, Conway. Haw! Haw!"

Also, Toby tiptoed out on the porch to see what was up. Toby is a little black and white dog with a little black tail and big pop eyes. Dad grabbed him by the tail, and you should have heard Toby howl.

Pa howled, too. "Never mind, cowards! Here's a customer! I'll just clip off this customer's tail; and if he's got a dollar, I'll shave him all over!"

There were some terrible howls. Our whole street echoed. Some howls came from Wilmer and Harley and me. We started running, and then I stopped. There was a howl from Archibald, and he was running, too.

23

"Well, look, Archibald," I said. "You don't have to die! It's only a joke. Even Toby knows it's a joke. Pa doesn't mean it. He just wants us to come. See. There are Kymie and Hanky and Corky on the porch. See? And Joel and Jerry, with the popsickles and the black hair. You don't have to come."

"Oh!" Archibald said. He put his hands in his pockets. "Excuse me," he said.

The big car moved up close, and Baker opened the door. Baker had a sort of purple suit, a cap with braid on it, and a big, anxious face. "Archibald," he said, "it's long past four o'clock. Do you wish to ask your new friends to tea?"

Archibald looked at Wilmer and Harley and me. He

said, "You can come to tea if you'll wash your hands."

"Tea!" Wilmer said. "We don't drink tea!"

"It isn't tea," Archibald said.

"If tea isn't tea," I said, "what is it?"

"Well, it's wafers and goat's milk."

Goat's milk.

"No, thanks," Harley said, turning pale. "Marines don't drink goat's milk."

So Archibald got into the car. "I'll see you," he said. "Come and see my doghouse sometime."

"Oh, sure," Wilmer Pitkin said. "Oh, sure."

The car rolled away.

"Well, we won't be bothered with Archibald again," I said. "He thought Pa meant it about Toby. He does not know about fun."

Wilmer moaned. "I wish good old Ralph was back. Ralph did not have someone like Baker breathing down his neck."

"Ralph did not drink goat's milk," Harley said. "We will never go to see Archibald at mealtime and get sick."

We wanted to bat a few, but it was too late. So we sat on my back porch, and Joel and Jerry and Hanky sat with us. Shannon was starting to cook his supper on the summer stove in the basement. Kymie was in the basement, too, getting his hair cut. We could hear him howling. Every time he howled, Pa would howl louder, and Toby would howl, too. And then Ma would yell from the kitchen, "Darlings, I'll come down there!"

"Let's plan a circus," I said. "There is going to be a vacation Thursday and Friday while the teachers go to a meeting. A circus would be fun."

But just then Pa began to yell, "Trent! Boy, if you don't leg it down here, I'm coming up there! And if I come, I'm going to shave every pumpkin head in sight. If I whack off an ear or two or some Marine's mustache, I won't charge for it!"

Harley felt of his lip. "Well," he said, "I'll be going."

He and Wilmer put their jackets over their heads and ran down the driveway. "Tell him we're some dear, dear girls, running away!" Harley yelled.

I went down to the basement. While Pa cut my hair, I told him all about Archibald and his best clothes and watch and ring.

"Well, clothes do not make the man," Pa said. "Look at me! Archibald might be a fine guy!"

"Sure," I said. "But can you see Archibald sliding into third in his good suit? Anyway, he does not know a joke from grim facts, Pa. He thought you meant it about Toby's tail. He thinks you are a corker, and we won't be bothered with him again."

CHAPTER III

The Sanitary Dog

But Tuesday morning Ma said, "Trenton, someone is waiting out in front of the house."

I knew it was Archibald Brewster.

"It's Brewster, the Ripper! Have the boys bring my horse to the alley, Kit!" I said.

"Blackie," Ma said, "you ain't runnin' away, be you?"

This is a game we play. Ma is Kit, and I am Blackie.

"You wouldn't leave me to face the Ripper alone, would you, Blackie?" Ma said. "After all we been through together?"

I began to back toward the kitchen door. "I'm desperate, Kit. I got to go. Kit, you talk to him. Tell him I hit the trail at sunup and headed toward Dodge."

"He won't believe me, Blackie. I ain't a good liar. Blackie, you got to face him."

Corky was listening and poking his breakfast Pop-O's around in the bowl. "That's that boy in his good suit," Corky said. "He wored it to school yesterday. Why did he wore it to school, Trent?"

I put my hands behind me and got hold of the doorknob. "So he could keep his hands in the pockets!" I said. "Good-by!"

Ma grabbed me, but I got away and ran out the back door. I flew down the alley and met Wilmer and Harley.

"Ma got me by the ear," I said. "I can still feel her fingerprints on it. I guess she wants us to be very chummy with Archibald and let him play on our team."

"This is bad," Wilmer said. "I can see the score in the big game now. Lawson Lions, 30. Brookfield Bumblebees, 6. Of course, I would bat four homers and bring each of you guys in once."

"Ha!" Harley said. "Maybe I would bat the homers. Maybe you would strike out, Pitkin. You always do."

"O. K., O. K.," Wilmer said. "Let's stop fooling around and hold a big meeting."

"The meeting is called to order," Harley said. "Let me think." He shut his eyes and tried to think hard. "Trent," he said, "you could have Toby bark at Archibald."

"I will do the thinking," Wilmer said. "Toby will not bark at a boy. A boy who is used to a dog would not be afraid of a little, worried-looking dog like Toby. Trent,

28

when is Kymie going to give a funeral? You could invite Archibald to help bury something. Maybe Archibald does not like funerals."

"Kymie does not have many customers for his cemetery now," I said. "Mrs. Miller has trapped all the mice that grew up in her mop closet, and the bat that lives behind our garage door has not departed. Kymie gave a funeral for a cricket on Saturday, and that is about as bad as things can get."

"Well," Harley said, "you could get your dad to cut Archibald's hair. Or you could invite him to supper and have him eat some of Shannon's cooking."

"Let Wilmer do the thinking," I said. "Shannon is a good cook."

"Yes," said Wilmer. "But the things he cooks are very queer. Archibald would not like them."

"Maybe you are right," I said.

Shannon cooks whatever he catches or fishes out of the water or pulls up out of the ground. Sometimes he does not know what it is. So if it is something that can wiggle, Shannon calls it chicken. If it can swim, he calls it fish. If it is something that grows in the ground, he calls it dandelion greens until he asks Ma.

"Ma looks at everything first," I said. "She tells Shannon whether it is O. K. to cook it or not. We Conways have rules at our house, and this is one of the rules."

When we got to school, Archibald's big car was there, and Archibald was getting out of it.

"Hi, Trenton!" he said. "I missed you!"

"Oh, that's O. K.," I said. "Are you going to play outfielder today and scramble through the thorny hedge if we lose the ball?" I had to invite him, to be polite.

"You can find your way," Wilmer said. "Good old Ralph left a trail of blood, and you can follow that."

"No, thanks," Archibald said. "I will observe."

Observe.

We did not ask him again, and he sat on the walk and watched us. Susie and Wanda and Glenora came over to talk to him and did not get their hopscotch game finished.

Glenora tried on Archibald's watch. Susie tried on his ring. Archibald said the brown stone was a tiger's eye.

While I was looking to see the ring, Wilmer struck me out.

"That was no strike!" I yelled. "Look, Pitkin, you know that was a ball!"

"It was a strike!" Wilmer yelled. "You're just like Ralph! I mean, good old Ralph was always mad, too, when a strike was called on him. You're out, Conway!"

"Oh, I am, am I?" I said. I dropped the bat, and Wilmer began to run. I chased him around the school three times, and then the bell rang.

Archibald walked into school with me. I was out of breath. "Well, Archibald," I said, "Puff! Puff! What do you think of baseball?"

"If that is baseball, I am sure it is the most fascinating game I've ever seen in all my life," said Archibald. *Fascinating.*

After school, Baker was waiting in the big car. "Come, Archibald," he said. "Your aunt is waiting to go shopping with you."

Archibald rode away waving at us, with his ring shining in the sun.

"Fascinating!" Wilmer said. "There he goes with his big words, the showoff! Don't let him know about our circus, Trent, or he will be right there. Observing."

The girls were listening in. "You boys ought to be ashamed," Wanda said. "Archibald is a poor, lonely boy."

"He is lonely, but he is not poor," Wilmer said. "His dad has two factories. You saw that car. You saw Baker. All that costs money."

I said, "So does goat's milk. I asked my dad. My dad says goats are very deceiving. They eat tar paper out of the rubbish heap, but when you pay for their milk you would think they eat at the Ritz. That is a big hotel. 'Give me good old honest cow's milk made of grass, any time,' my dad says."

"Well, money isn't everything," Glenora said. "Money is nothing if you're lonely." She fluttered her black eyelashes. "Haven't you ever been lonely, Harley?"

"Not for girls!" Harley said.

I said, "Archibald has his father's aunt, and Baker, and a dog."

31

"Trent Conway, would you trade with him?" Wanda asked me. "Would you live with Baker and the dog and Archibald's father's aunt, and let Archibald live with your six brothers?"

"Well," I said, "my six brothers would not like this."

"No, they would not!" Wilmer said. "We're getting up a circus in Trent's back yard. Anyway, Archibald lives where he belongs."

"Archibald went to see you, Trent," Wanda said. "Did you go to see him?"

"It is only manners," Susie said, "to go to see a new neighbor."

"Manners. You don't think we have manners," I said. "I'll show you we've got manners. We'll go to see Archibald this very night."

"You'd better go home and wash first," Wanda said.

"Why?" asked Harley.

"Because Archibald is very sanitary. His aunt is very sanitary. His dog is probably sanitary. So clean up if you're going to see Archibald."

"Ha!" I said. "We are going to see Archibald, but he is not going to see *us*, and neither is his sanitary aunt."

We went down the alley between Oak Street and Caroline. Good old Ralph used to live in a yellow house on Caroline, and his house looked very empty and lonely as we passed by.

"My dad says it will stay empty," I said. "No one will move to Brookfield until there are more jobs."

We cut across the corner lot to Dennis Place. Dennis Place runs back of Maxwell, and Wilmer's Aunt Harriet lives there. She has a tall tree that is easy to climb if you know how. First, you climb the fence. Then you crawl up on the garage and flop down on your stomach and wiggle-waggle across the garage roof to the other edge. Then you crawl into the tree.

From the tree we could see all over the neighborhood. We could see Archibald's yard behind his big house.

"There's the doghouse!" I said. "And look at that dog!"

"He's big as a bear!" Harley said. "Oh-Oh! There's Archibald, home from his shopping trip. He's coming to play with his dog."

But Baker came with a dish. Baker fed the dog. Archibald only observed the way he observed our ball games.

Then he walked around the yard, slowly, looking at things. He is as big as I am, but he looked little from the tree. He did not touch anything. He started to go back to the house.

That was when I whistled. I did not know why.

Archibald turned around and saw us in the tree. He ran down to the fence and called to us. "What are you doing up there?"

"We came to see your dog," Wilmer said.

"Then come down and see him!" Archibald yelled. "There's a back gate."

So we wiggle-waggled back across the garage and shinnied down the fence, and Archibald opened his gate.

"Come on," he said. "Nero is out of his house. Don't get too close."

"He's *bigger* than a bear!" Harley said.

The dog was black and shiny. He had a long nose. He wrinkled this nose and showed us his teeth, and he was not smiling.

"My aunt bought him from a kennel," Archibald said. "He is a very fine dog, but fine dogs are nervous. Don't get near him."

Nero growled. Archibald shoved his hands deep down in his pockets.

"Can't you play with him?" Wilmer asked.

"Don't stand close," Archibald said. "A dog is not a plaything."

"Well," I said, "that is news to me. That would be news to my six brothers."

"It's news to me, too" said Wilmer. "My dog, Scooter, sleeps with me."

"Our dog, Toby, takes turns sleeping with us," I said. "Don't tell Ma."

"That is very unsanitary," said Archibald. "What about germs?"

"Oh, Toby isn't particular," I said. "Well, we'd better be going."

We climbed the tree and wiggle-waggled across the garage and shinnied down the fence and ran through the corner lot to Caroline Street and down the alley to Oak Street.

Wilmer said, "Archibald's garage is almost as big as our house. He is too rich for us."

"Also he is too sanitary," Harley said. "He keeps his hands in his pockets so that he will not touch anything dirty."

"Well," I said, "my mother believes in germs, too. If she sees Archibald very close, she will want me to be clean and shiny like him."

"Don't let him come to your house," said Wilmer and Harley. "We can't be bothered with him."

"He will have to play hopscotch with Wonderful Wanda," Harley said.

"I wish Ralph Jackson was back," I said. "Good old Ralph didn't mind a little dirt and a few germs wiggling around."

"Right!" said Wilmer. "And he could play baseball. The Lions would not beat us if Ralph were here instead of Archibald. Victor Valley is a hard man, but he was afraid of good old Ralph."

CHAPTER IV

Archibald Observes

The circus was going to be on Thursday, so we had to get away from Archibald on Wednesday to do some planning and rehearsing.

We did this in my back yard because that is where we have our circuses.

We planned some keen acts. Some of them, like our big magic act, we had done before. I was Presto the Magician. My helper was Petro. Together we did a very great disappearing act. We always do it the same way.

We have a box and a barrel from Sensenbrenner's Grocery. The barrel is over beside the garage. The box is in the middle of the yard with the open side turned toward the audience.

Joel is Petro. He crawls into the box and sits in it so that everyone can see him.

Then I throw a scarf down over the box. At the back of the box is a loose board. While I give the audience some very fast talk, Joel slips out of the box and puts the board back in place.

Then he lies flat on the ground behind the box, out of sight.

Presto! I whisk away the scarf, and the box is empty. That is when the girls always scream.

I look for Petro. I am very worried, and I keep talking. "Oh, what if that dear boy and his new ten-dollar shoes have disappeared into outer space?" I wring my hands. "Maybe he has gone into orbit! Oh, woe is me! Woe, woe! What will I tell his loving mother when we see him zooming and beep-beeping across the sky at bedtime?"

I cry and wipe my eyes on my sleeves, and then I call, "Oh, Petro, my dear boy, please make some feeble answer! Petro!"

"Here I am, Presto!" someone shouts. Jerry pops up out of the barrel, looking just like Joel.

The audience screams and laughs and claps, and no one ever seems to know that it is Joel who hides in the box and Jerry who pops out of the barrel.

Shannon and Hanky had a very keen act, but they had a little trouble rehearsing. Shannon was a lion tamer, and Hanky was the lion. Hanky has a lion suit that Ma made for him. Shannon had Pa's old high hat and a chair and a whip.

"You remember," Hanky said, "that whip is only for looks, not for action."

"Get going!" Shannon said. "When I crack this whip, you're supposed to hop up on a stool and roar."

"Where is the candy?" Hanky said.

"Candy?" Shannon said. "That is only for the circus, not for rehearsal." He cracked the whip.

But Hanky sat still. He reached around, took hold of his rope tail, and tickled his chin with it. "H'm! H'm!" he sang.

"Hurry up!" Shannon said. "You are supposed to hop up on the stool."

"Oh, that is for the circus," Hanky said. "Not for rehearsal."

"O. K.," I said. "Cut the stalling! Remember, the customers are going to pay a nickel to see this circus, and they expect to see some very good acts. Kymie, you had better put Toby through his tricks."

Toby can speak and roll over and play dead. As soon as he had done all three, Kymie gave him some candy.

"What's the idea?" Hanky said. "That performer is getting candy!"

"He is only a dog," I said. "He does not understand that this is only rehearsal."

Shannon said, "Hanky, if you wish to roll over and play dead, you will get some candy, too."

Hanky hopped up on his stool and roared.

We also had a keen tumbling act. Harley and Wilmer and the twins and I were in it. Corky was going to be in it, but Ma came out on the porch.

"What are you trying to do to Corky?" she yelled.

"Mom, we are only going to put him up on Joel's feet!"

"Not while I'm alive!" Ma said. "I have managed to keep seven Conway twisters all in one piece all these years, and I am not going to lose one that way."

"That's O. K., Mrs. Conway," Wilmer said. "Scooter can take his place. Come here, Scooter."

But Scooter put his tail between his legs and ran home as fast as he could, ki-yi-ing all the way.

Ma laughed. "Scooter has better sense than some people I know!" she said.

But the tumbling act was good, and so were the trapeze acts we practiced on our swing.

When the acts were all ready, we went to Sensenbrenner's Grocery and got a big Pop-O box to make a ticket booth. We carried it home over our heads. Harley walked ahead to keep us from bumping into anyone. We did not have any streets to cross. We just walked around the block singing "The Marines' Hymn."

We heard a car pass, and Harley said, "That was Baker taking Archibald and his aunt somewhere. You should have seen them stare."

"It's O. K.," I said. "They did not know us with this box over our heads."

"I am glad," Wilmer said. "We cannot have Archibald and his aunt at the circus."

"We do not need their nickels," Harley said.

The next day was Circus Day, and all the girls came. Archibald was not there.

"You boys should be ashamed," Wanda said. "You are very unkind to Archibald, and it is only because he is not Ralph Jackson."

"Good old Ralph was our friend," I said. "Do you see that carving on Ma's clothes pole? Ralph did that. It was the first carving he did with his birthday knife."

"And the last," said Susie Scott. "He carved some of her clothesline, too."

"Well," I said, "if the customers will kindly sit on the back porch and stop making remarks about dear departed friends, we will start the circus."

My brother Kymie was the barker. "Atten-SHUN, ladies and gentlemen!" Kymie yelled. "All ready for the greatest circus side show of any circus side show under one stretch of canvas! Fearless Shannon and his fierce, man-eating lion!"

Right then my mother opened the kitchen door. "Trenton," she said, "you have another guest."

Archibald Brewster was standing there all dressed up, with a dollar in his hand.

"O. K.," I said. "I believe I can change that."

I went over to the Pop-O box ticket booth. I could feel the guys poking nickels into my back pocket. When

I reached in, I was very happy to find ninety-five cents where there had been only eighty.

I took Archibald's dollar and gave him the ninety-five cents. Then I dusted a spot on the porch with my sleeve.

"There you are, sir," I said. "Sit right down, sir, and you will see the most circus you ever saw, sir."

"I have seen some very fine circuses," Archibald said.

"Well," Wilmer said, "this is the most you ever saw for a nickel."

Shannon and Hanky did their act. Presto the Magician and the Famous Disappearing Act came next. Toby did all his tricks. Wilmer's dog, Scooter, and Harley's dog, Bingo, did theirs, and then Bingo chased his tail until he was dizzy.

Harley and Wilmer and the twins and I did our tumbling act. We borrowed Corky's teddy bear to be the top man and paid Corky a nickel.

It was a keen circus, and when we were through we had popcorn and some pink lemonade that Ma made, and some cookies that Shannon made from Miss Honeychurch's recipe. Miss Honeychurch is Shannon's teacher, and he has a very big case on her.

Harley said, "Well, Archibald, how did you like the circus?"

Susie said, "It was very silly! Trent, it is time Toby learned a new trick."

"That's right!" said Glenora. "Any dog can roll over and play dead. Besides, Toby's lazy. He stayed dead so long this time that Kymie ran and got his spade."

"Toby went to sleep," Susie said. "He was bored. So was I. I almost went to sleep, too." She yawned so wide that we could all see her tonsils.

"The disappearing act is very corny," Wanda said. "Everybody knows that Jerry hides behind the box and Joel comes out of the barrel. Besides, Jerry's sweater is red today, and Joel's is green."

"So they forgot to dress alike," I said. "What do you expect for a nickel? Anyway, it was Jerry in the barrel."

"It was very boring," said Susie. "Ho-hum!"

The talk was only because Archibald was there. The girls always liked the circus before. Wanda never understood the disappearing act before. And they were always afraid of the fierce lion before.

"Boring!" I said. "Oh, indeed! Indeed! Well, perhaps you would like your money back. All the cheapskates who are not satisfied will please sneak past the ticket booth and receive your nickel back."

Then I remembered that the nickels were gone. My blue china piggy bank was standing there, looking something like Wanda with its blue eyes; and there were no nickels in it.

"Of course," I said, "I have only folding money. Archibald, can you change a dollar?"

"Certainly," said Archibald.

Certainly.

He took two fifty cent pieces out of his pocket.

"On second thought," I said, "we did not promise to give your money back. You saw this show at your own risk. Good-by."

So the girls went home, but Archibald still sat there. "Doesn't a real circus ever come to this town?" he asked.

"You know our town is too small," I said. "I told you that my dad says we need more business in Brookfield. There are no big factories, and there are not enough places to work."

"My dad is going to build a new factory in some town," Archibald said. "It will be a canning factory. We will live where the new factory is when my mother is well. I have been waiting a long time."

"Well," Wilmer said, "if you are going to wait for your nickel, I guess we can dig one up for you so you can go home."

"I am not going home," said Archibald. "I am going to stay here. Trenton's mother very kindly invited me to dinner."

Dinner.

"It's supper," I said. "Down, Toby!"

Toby was sniffing Archibald and looking very worried, and I couldn't blame him. Toby never saw a boy dressed like Archibald except on Sunday.

Well, we wanted to play baseball, but we did not want Archibald to think he was a Bumblebee. We wished he would go home but I have some manners.

"I am very glad you are staying, Archibald," I said.

"We are having chops. Ma said she believed they were made from pigtails, but they were the best Mr. Sensenbrenner could do today. I hope you'll like them."

"I shall," said Archibald.

That did not work. Harley gave me a sad wink that meant, "We are going to see him on the ball team yet!"

"Well," I said, "do you wish to wrestle, Archibald? We will be careful not to tear your best clothes much. Down, Toby! Can't you see that Archibald's dressed up? There isn't a flea on him! Want to wrestle, Archibald?"

"No, thanks," Archibald said. "I shall observe."

So we wrestled. I got Wilmer Pitkin down, and I was sitting on his chest. "Do you beg?" I said.

"Look!" Wilmer said. "Look at Archibald!"

Toby was on Archibald's lap giving him a big, sloppy kiss on the cheek. Archibald was scared. He was bending way back looking at Toby with his eyes crossed. His hands were in his pockets.

"Toby!" I yelled. "Down! Don't you know when a man is only observing? Down!"

Just then Wilmer gave a heave and rolled me over. The next minute he was sitting on me, and it was Archibald's fault.

Then Pa drove the station wagon into the garage and came out and made a speech. "Well," he said, "the bat is still there behind the door. But I'll keep hoping!"

He went into the house, and Ma called us to supper; so Wilmer and Harley went home.

45

"Archibald," Ma said, "I put out a guest towel for you. You may wash first." While the washbowl was clean and the soap was not soaked, she meant.

"Ma," Joel said, "don't drag Archibald up to the bathroom. He hasn't touched anything with germs squirming around on it. He hasn't touched a thing! "

But Archibald wanted to wash even if it was a waste of soap. "Thank you, Mrs. Conway," he said very politely. "Trent, will you please show me the bathroom?"

He came down smelling of soap. His hair was combed slick. Corky was next, then Joel and Jerry, then Hanky and Kymie, then Shannon, then me.

"Do you always start with the youngest?" Archibald said.

"Right!" I said. "Each older guy can clean up a little after the one before him. We have rules, and this is one of them."

Right then Shannon skidded past us in his blue apron with a fry-pan in one hand and a salt shaker in the other. "Forgot my grease," he said.

"Where is he going?" Archibald asked.

"Oh," I said, "he's been out running and jumping after his supper. Now he is going to the basement to cook what he caught. What's for supper, Shannon?"

"Frog legs." Shannon smacked. "I've only got two."

"Well, I do not eat frogs. Invite me when you have chicken," I said.

Then Ma called us to the table, and we said grace.

46

After that, Pa gave Archibald a big smile. "Well," Pa
said, "Supper! Supper! All pitch in, for Old Dan Tucker!"

"Daddy!" Ma said. "Maybe Archibald will not appre-
ciate your jokes, darling. Maybe he is used to rules of
table etiquette."

Etiquette.

She meant manners.

"Archibald," Pa said, "we have a rule, too. Don't you
ever think we haven't! Every man is allowed both elbows
and one knee on the table, but no more. So don't you
try anything funny."

Everybody laughed except Archibald. Now maybe he
will stay away, I thought.

47

Archibald had very fine manners. Ma gave him a big napkin. He unfolded it half and laid it across his pants. He cut his chops with his knife and ate them with his fork.

Corky watched him eat.

"Come, come, Corky, man!" Pa said. "Let me cut up that chop, and you get going. If you don't eat, I'm going to adopt me a boy who will."

So everybody had a good supper, and Shannon got to the table in time to eat the last two chops and some apple pie.

"Archibald," Ma said, "would you like another piece of pie?"

But just then we heard a horn.

"Anybody expecting a car with a driver in uniform?" Dad asked. "Are you, Corky? You, Hank? Kymie?"

"That's Baker," said Archibald. "Mrs. Conway, will you please excuse me? And thank you for the very lovely dinner."

"This was supper," Joel said. "Dinner is at noon."

"Excuse me," Archibald said. "Mrs. Conway, thank you for the lovely supper."

Then Archibald rode away in his long car. "That's that!" I said. "Archibald will be very glad to get back to his sanitary house where they have dinner at night. We will not be bothered with him again."

CHAPTER V

Just a Little Wrestling

At seven o'clock on Friday morning Ma said, "My stars! See who's sitting on the front porch!"

It was Archibald. He was sitting hunched up like a puppy, waiting. I opened the door a little and said, "Did you forget something?"

Archibald stood up. He said, "Good morning, Trenton. I returned to thank your mother properly."

I was going to say, "You're welcome, I'm sure," and shut the door.

But Ma was breathing down my neck. "Come in, Archibald," she said. "Breakfast is ready. Do you like wheat cakes and syrup?"

"I think so, thank you," Archibald said.

"You think so!" Pa said. "Man we want the facts of the case. But remember, everything you say may be used against you."

Archibald's eyes popped like Toby's, and he looked scared to death. I thought he would run out the door, and we would get rid of him; but Shannon had to say something.

"Don't die, Archibald," he said. "Pa is just practicing for court. He always practices on us. Law and barbering."

"And there's not much money in either," Pa said.

So Archibald gave facts. He said, "I have seen many pictures of pancakes, but I have never eaten any."

"Well," Pa said, "you sit right down here and stash away as many of these flapjacks as you can. But don't go over thirty for the first time. Here. Take some maple syrup."

"It's pure maple, mixed with brown sugar," Shannon said. "I made it."

So Archibald started out easy with six wheat cakes. Then he ate four more, and then three more.

"That's thirteen," Hanky said. "That's very unlucky! Here. Take two of mine. They're getting salty, anyway."

Archibald turned red. "You don't need to turn red," Kymie said. "Hanky only means that he has eaten too many."

So Archibald ate two more.

"More, Archibald?" Ma said.

"No, thank you, Mrs. Conway," Archibald said. "I have eaten—I have eaten—I mean, they are getting salty!"

It sounded so funny when Archibald said it that everyone laughed, and Toby barked.

"Off the noise!" Pa said. "Order in the court! When I come home today, I want to see the back yard and basement looking slick as a button. Remember! I don't want the neighbors saying that Attorney and Mrs. Trenton J. Conway, Senior, have a dirty yard and basement and eight big, lazy boys."

"Seven, Pa!" Jerry said. "Seven big, lazy boys."

Pa pointed at each of us and counted. "One! Two! Three! Four! Five! Six! Seven! Eight big, lazy boys!"

"Ha!" Joel said. "You counted Archibald Brewster!"

Pa looked at us. "Which one is Archibald Brewster? I didn't know one of my big lazy boys was named Archibald Brewster."

Archibald said, "I am Archibald Brewster, sir." His voice squeaked a little. "I thought you knew it."

"A-ha!" Pa said. "That was before eight o'clock on the morning of the seventeenth! Since then, everything has changed. When I make out my tax paper, can I write, 'Dear Uncle Sam: At eight o'clock on the morning of the seventeenth, one Archibald Brewster lapped up twenty-thirty of my flapjacks, with pure maple syrup, and I demand a deduction'? No. I cannot! I will simply write: 'Exemptions: eight big, lazy boys!'"

Right then the telephone rang, and Pa went to answer. So Hanky poked Archibald. "Joke!" Hanky said.

Archibald tried to giggle with his mouth closed because that is polite.

After a while Pa took his hat and briefcase and we heard him tell Ma good-by. He also said a few words to the bat behind the garage door. Then he raced the motor and drove away in the station wagon.

After breakfast we sat on the porch. "Trent," Archibald said, "did good old Ralph ever eat here?"

"Hundreds of times," I said. "Sometimes he ate Ma's cooking. Sometimes he ate Shannon's."

"Did he wash first?" Archibald said.

"Well," I said, "sometimes his paws looked more as if he only wiped them a little on his pants."

"I mean, did he have first turn?"

"No," I said. "Ralph washed with me."

"I see," Archibald said. "Did he have a guest towel?"

"No," I said. "Ralph did not care for a guest towel with pink daisies on it. What was good enough for me was good enough for him. Good old Ralph used my towel."

"Oh!" Archibald said. "Well, I was just thinking about it."

I wondered if he was going to try to stay for dinner. "Archibald," I said, "what are you doing today?"

"Whatever you do," he said.

I wanted to play ball, but I had to keep Archibald out of that.

"Well," I said, "every day can't be circus day. We will omit the basement, but we will have to clean the yard. You could observe, but it would not be much fun."

"No," Archibald said, "it would not." But he did not go.

Toby slipped up, sniffed Archibald's ear, and then smacked him across the face. Archibald shuddered a little, but he gave Toby a quick little pat.

"You will get dirty," I said. "Toby played with a toad in the garden this morning."

Archibald shuddered again and stood up.

"You could help me clean the yard," I said. "But you can't clean the yard in those clothes. What are you looking at?"

Archibald was staring up toward the sky with his eyes and mouth wide open.

"Don't faint, Archibald," I said. "The little angels are not sliding down from the sky. Kymie and Hanky are just coming down from their room."

Kymie and Hanky slid down the porch post onto the ground. Shannon came behind them.

"I made your bed, Trent," Shannon said. "I did not snoop under your pillow. But Ma came up sniffing around!"

I moaned. "I was going to have some candied orange peels. That's why I was saving them," I said.

"Well, Ma is mad, and she sent you some orders," Shannon said. "You are ordered to mow the yard."

"How can I when I have company?" I said. "Shannon, you can mow. Kymie, you can clip the roses. Hanky, you can rake."

But just then Wilmer Pitkin and Harley Scott came along wanting to bat a few. Of course they were very surprised to see Archibald sitting there with me.

"Hi, Trent!" they said. "Did you hear anything from good old Ralph? Hi, Archibald!"

Wilmer said, "Trent, it is a very nice morning for wrestling, but I notice you have company."

"Yes," Harley said, "it is not polite to have a lot of fun wrestling when you have company."

"Of course," Wilmer said, "we do not have any company, so we can have some fun. Come on, Harley."

So Wilmer and Harley and Shannon and Kymie and Hanky went out to wrestle in my back yard.

"Archibald," I said, "maybe you would like to scuffle with Joel and Jerry. They would not rough you up much."

I thought he would get mad and go home, but he said, "I will wrestle with you. Let me take my things out of my pockets."

I emptied my pockets, too. I took out my gum, my dried grasshopper, my horse chestnut, my compass, my rubber bands, my nails, my electric cord, and my flashlight.

Archibald took out a white handkerchief with his initial on it. Then he took out a comb, a pen, a pencil, and a zipper purse. Last he took out two dear little books.

"What are they?" I said.

"One is my pocket dictionary," Archibald said. "The other is a little book of rules for wrestling."

Rules.

"Well," I said, "Take off your watch and ring, and I will show you how to wrestle."

We walked out to the middle of our back yard. I took a very light hold on Archibald's knees and got ready to throw him very gently.

But something happened. I mean, the next minute I was down, and Archibald was on top of me.

"Very funny!" I said. "What's the idea of falling on me and holding me down on my back? Let me up so we can start wrestling."

"I have started," Archibald said. He got up.

I got up, and he grabbed me. He grabbed me some very sly way, and I slipped off my feet. The next thing I knew, I was right back on the ground and Archibald was holding me down.

Was I mad! "Hey!" I said. "What's the idea, throwing me down?"

"We're wrestling, aren't we?" said Archibald.

"Well, sure," I said, "but you threw me down before I could get started."

Archibald smiled. "Get up if you can," he said.

Wilmer and Harley and Shannon and Kymie and

Hanky were standing in a circle around us, looking at us.

Wilmer said, "How can Trent get up, the way you're holding him down? You don't wrestle fair, Archibald. Let me show you how to wrestle."

"Fine!" said Archibald. "Are you ready?"

"You bet I'm ready! Ooooops! Ow!" Wilmer said. "Hey, what's the idea, throwing me down when I'm trying to show you how to wrestle?"

"Yeah," Harley said. "Let Pitkin get up, Archibald."

"Certainly," Archibald said. He stood up and slapped his hands together. "Do you wish to wrestle, Harley?"

Harley just stuck out his jaw and grabbed Archibald's legs. The next minute they were both down on the ground, and we heard someone laughing.

It was Pa. He had come back for Ma's letter that he forgot. "Archibald fell on me, Mr. Conway," Harley said. "He's very awkward."

Dad walked all around them and looked at them, while Harley tried to get up. "You certainly are awkward, Archibald," Pa said. "As grandpa would say, you fell on that boy so that he's four points down. How did you learn to be so awkward?" He winked at Archibald.

Archibald tried to wink back. "I learned it in my book of rules, sir," he said.

Just then Ma called from the kitchen door. "Darling, I think I sent you on an errand."

"Oh, yes," Pa said. "Trent, call up the army and the navy and get this lawn cleaned up today! Or else!"

Pa went away, and Archibald got up, and then Harley got up. Harley's face was very red.

"Well," Harley said, "I have to go. But there is one thing I wish to say to you, Archibald. I could not wrestle you because I was afraid I would soil your best clothes."

"Me, too," said Wilmer. "I was afraid I would tear your white shirt."

"I have more clothes like these at home," said Archibald.

"Well," I said, "they are too good to wrestle in, so I will not wrestle with you until you get some others."

Then Shannon had to get smart. He said, "You guys had better not wrestle with Archibald until you study his rule book."

"O.K., Smarty," I said. "Let's get at this yard."

"Well," Wilmer and Harley said, "we just stopped to see if you had heard from good old Ralph, Trent. We will be going."

But they waited. They thought Archibald would go.

"Trenton," Archibald said, "did good old Ralph help clean your lawn?"

"Ralph could rake as well as he could bat," I said.

Archibald rolled up his white sleeves. "I will help you clean the lawn," he said.

But Baker drove up and parked the long car and started to get out. We ran around to the street.

"Oh, there you are, Archibald!" Baker said. "Your aunt wishes you to come home and practice your piano lesson before luncheon." '

Luncheon.

"But, Baker," Archibald said, "I promised Trent I would clean his lawn."

Baker peeked into the back yard. "What in the world hit that yard?" he said.

"Well," Archibald said, "we had a circus yesterday. And we wrestled a little this morning."

We. Next he will be saying, *we* play the Lawson Lions three weeks from Tuesday, I thought.

Baker was still peering into the yard. "What are those

queer objects on the ground just beyond the garage?"

"Just graves," I said. "That is where my brother Kymie buries whoever departs."

"I see," Baker said. I thought he shuddered a little, but I wasn't sure. "Well, come along, Archibald," he said. "Your friend will excuse you."

"Sure," I said. "You'd better practice your piano lesson, Archibald."

So Archibald got in the long car and rode away. He did not look back and wave.

Wilmer and Harley and I sat on the back step with my brothers, and we had a talk.

"I have news for you guys," Wilmer said. "Archibald pinned you. Of course, it is only because he's awkward, I hope! But he pinned you."

"How about you, Pitkin?" Harley said. "He had you down, and you could not wiggle."

"I could, too," Wilmer said. "I could wiggle my ears."

"Well," I said, "I am glad Wonderful Wanda and Gorgeous Glenora and Susie and the other girls did not see that. They would not believe it was because Archibald is awkward. Also, I wish he would stop pestering around my house. I do not know any way to get rid of him."

Wilmer is a very great thinker. "Archibald does not walk very much," he said. "He rides everywhere in that big car. When he comes around again, let's take him for a very long walk."

"A very good idea," I said. "His shoes are thin, and shiny, too. He will be glad to stay at home and rest his feet and polish his shoes after a long walk."

So Wilmer and Harley went away, and we Conways slaved all day Friday and most of Saturday until the yard was clean. I almost wished Archibald had stayed to help.

Saturday night Ma said, "Darlings, you forgot the basement, but I did not forget. Some day there is going to be a very big blow-up around Oak Street if that basement does not get cleaned."

CHAPTER VI

Chickens and Beet Greens

The next week the girls were very bossy. They wanted to tell us what to do.

Wonderful Wanda started it. She said, "I suppose you boys have learned a few manners from Archibald."

"We know enough manners," Wilmer said. "We know enough to say good morning and good-by to Miss Kramer and 'Excuse me!' if we bump into Miss Buckmaster."

"Very sweet," said Susie Scott. "You know how to treat the teachers."

"We know enough to pass the salted peanuts around, cousin; and not to eat them before the hungry people of the world, cousin," Harley said.

"Well, O.K., cousin," said Susie. "Take some. But I

have only a few. Wait. I know you very well, cousin. Let me kiss the bag good-by."

So Susie kissed the bag with a big smack, and then she passed it. She was right. There were only enough peanuts for Wilmer and Harley and me, so Harley blew the bag up and popped it.

Glenora said, "It is very easy to be polite to your old friends, but you are not polite to your new one. It is rude for you boys to play baseball day after day and not invite Archibald to play."

"Baseball is not Archibald's game," I said. "He only wishes to observe."

"He has observed for days and days," said Glenora. "He must have learned to play a little."

"A little is not enough," said Wilmer. "I am a very great thinker, and I have thought about this a lot. Our mothers will come to watch the big game. It would be a terrible disgrace to lose the game and let Victor Valley laugh at us, all because Archibald had his hands in his pockets and could not catch the ball."

Wanda shook back her yellow pony tails. She said, "It is better to lose the game than to be impolite."

"No one but a girl would make that statement," Wilmer said. "This talk is now ended."

But when the girls had gone, Wilmer said, "I know the girls. They will tell Archibald to tell Miss Kramer that he wants to play. It is time to take him for that walk."

We decided to take the long walk on Saturday. I was

elected to take the lunch for all the group and Archibald."

Saturday morning I found Ma in the kitchen. Breakfast was over, and the sink drain was plugged up. Pa was trying to open it with a tool called a plumber's helper. It is a rubber suction cup on the end of a long stick.

I watched a while, and Pa said, "It looks as if I am going out to sea. Trent, do you know how to work this thing?"

"Of course," I said. "We studied all about it in science."

"Well, Professor Conway," Pa said, "how would you like to put your great learning into practice?"

"Just a minute!" Ma said. "That job takes more muscle than science, and muscle is what you've got, Mr. Conway."

"Well," Pa said, "you'll admit it was a nice try!" He pushed once more. The drain took a big, deep swallow, and down went all the water.

"Thar she blows!" I said.

Pa turned around and made a big bow to Ma. "Congratulations, Duchess," he said. "The House of Conway will never want for bread. If all else fails, I can always take this trusty plumber's helper and get a job!"

"I'll clean up," Ma said.

I said, "I'll help you."

Pa stopped at the door and stared at me. Ma was surprised, too.

I grinned at her. "Kit," I said, "while I mop up, pack me rations for five. I'm ridin' today."

"Ridin'?" Ma said. "You never told me, Blackie."

"I never knowed it till sunup, Kit," I said. "But we aim to reach Turner Ranch by noon."

"That's a long ways, Blackie."

"We're traveling fast, Kit," I said. "Fast."

"Who's a-going, Blackie?"

"Scott and Pitkin and the Kid, Shannon."

"Ye said five, Blackie."

"We're takin' the city slicker. He don't count."

"With him along, you ain't never going to reach Turner Ranch, Blackie."

"Four of us will make it, Kit." Then I giggled. I couldn't help it. I said, "Maybe Archibald will phone Baker to pick him up because his shoes are all worn out."

"Trent Conway," Ma said, "are you playing some mean trick on Archibald?"

"Well, look," I said. "The big game is two weeks from Tuesday. We're just going to keep walking until Archibald gets a little bit tired and does not wish to play ball. That's all."

"Mr. Conway," Ma said, "what do you think of that?"

"It is an old trick," Pa said. "We used to take the visiting city boys for a walk in Callahan's Woods. It was the strangest thing, but the city slickers always seemed to get lost, and we would have to come back without them.

Of course they were always found. Ah, we were gay lads! A merry, mad company! Of course, that was in the dear, dead days beyond recall, before my troubles all began."

"*Mister* Conway!" Ma said, very loud. "So you were mad and merry, were you? And your troubles did not begin until you met me?" Then in a very different voice she said, "Darling, you may open the defense, and you'd better make it good."

"Darling," Pa said, "don't misunderstand. I only *thought* I was happy in those days. I did not know my own misery. My true happiness came only after I had you and our seven fine sons." Pa bowed. "The defense rests. Excuse me. I will hasten away to my more-or-less honest toil."

He gave Ma a kiss on the cheek and went off to the garage, singing. "Oh, when I was single, I made the money jingle. . . . "

Mrs. Miller, next door, popped her head out and laughed.

"I'll get him!" Ma said through her teeth. Then she laughed, too, and went over to look at the beetles on Mrs. Miller's roses, and I knew she was not mad.

She packed me some sandwiches and cookies. When she finished, Archibald was sitting on the front porch with Shannon and Toby, and I had a surprise.

Archibald was not wearing his shiny shoes. He was wearing some boots with thick soles. He had a sweater on over his shirt and he had a little pack on his back.

"Are you saving your good shoes?" I said.

"No," he said. "These are my hiking boots."

"What's in the pack?" Shannon asked. "It looks like a Scout pack."

"It has a few first aid things we might need," Archibald said. "Aunt Grace suggested it."

Suggested.

"We have a lunch," I said. "That's all we need."

But Archibald took his pack.

We met Harley and Wilmer and began our hike.

"Fast or slow?" Archibald said.

"Double quick!" Harley said. "Naturally. Marines always march double quick."

So we walked out to the Military Road in twelve minutes, and that is one mile. Harley and Toby were panting.

"I thought you said we would walk fast," Archibald said. "What are you slowing down for?"

"We're hungry," I said. "After all, we have walked a mile."

So we sat under a tree. Archibald opened his first aid kit, and I thought he would take out bandages and pills and corn plasters.

But he took out a thermos bottle of lemonade and some paper cups.

"First aid!" he said. "I made it myself. Supper, supper! All pitch in, for Old Dan Tucker!"

We ate the sandwiches and cookies and drank the lemonade.

Then we started down Military Road, which is a side road, and after a while we met a white chicken running for its life.

Toby barked, but I held his leash tight.

"Very delicious-looking chicken," Shannon said. He smacked.

"Oh-oh! I should have brought a leash for you!" I said.

"Here comes another chicken!" Wilmer yelled. "See her run! She must be late to the chicken convention."

Harley pulled his jacket up over his head and jumped and yelled, "Shoo!"

The chicken squawked and ran faster, flapping her wings and kicking up the dust.

While we were laughing at her, Archibald said, "Here comes the flock!"

Sure enough, there were chickens all over the road ahead of us. They were flying low, just letting their toes touch the ground, and squawking as loud as they could squawk.

Then we saw a car over on the main road. "That's Mr. Turner!" I said. "He's yelling at us!"

The car stopped and we ran across the corner of a field, to the main road.

"Boys, can you help me round up those chickens?" Mr. Turner asked. "Someone left a gate open, and the hens got out. Someone else set a dog on them, and now they're

scared. If you'll hop in the car, we'll drive out beyond
them. Then if you boys can sort of scatter, I think we can
head them off and start them back toward the ranch."
He winked. "You can earn a good dinner. Chickens are
very grateful for favors!"

"That's a deal, Mr. Turner!" Wilmer said.

It worked, too. It was just like heading off cattle on
the range, only I think we made more noise.

The chickens squawked louder than wild geese and
tried to get past us, but we let them know we were tough.

Soon we had them headed back toward the ranch,
and then we ran into trouble. About twenty chickens
turned and headed for the swamp.

"We'll have to forget them for now!" Mr. Turner

shouted to the boys, "We can't get in there to head them off!"

"Toby can do it!" Archibald said. "I can make it into the swamp in these boots and tell Toby to chase them out!"

He grabbed the leash and was off.

That worked, too. Toby is little, and he does not have much chance to show off; but he is a very smart dog. He raced around and barked, and the chickens ran out toward the side road, flapping and squawking.

"Some dog!" Wilmer said. "Of course, Scooter could have chased them faster, but Toby is doing O. K."

Archibald came up, puffing and grinning. He wiped his face with a white handkerchief.

And then a funny thing happened. Archibald hunched down beside Toby and patted him all over. "Good Toby!" he kept saying. "Good old Toby!" Toby smacked all over his face.

"He played with a toad again this morning," I said.

"Toads are not so bad," Archibald said, and he gave Toby a big hug.

"Aw, cut the mush!" I said. "Come on! We're not through with the round-up yet."

In a few more minutes we had all the hens in the field between the garden and the chicken run.

And then Shannon got us into trouble. It is very hard for Shannon to pass little green growing things and not get to thinking about some recipe. He stopped and stared at the garden and licked his lips.

"Come on!" I said, "This is no time to stare!"

"But look at those dandelion greens!"

"Come on!" I said.

The chickens were glad to get back into a place that they knew. They crowded through their gate and then kept fluttering around inside the chicken run.

Mr. Turner laughed. "Those old biddies will have something to talk about for days!" he said. Then he reached in his pocket for his billfold. "How about a little folding money, men?" He gave each of us a dollar.

Archibald began, "Oh, we don't need this!"

But the rest of us yelled "Thank you!" so loud that Mr. Turner didn't hear him.

Then Shannon smiled very sweetly. "Mr. Turner, you said something about dinner."

For a minute I could taste chicken. I was very proud to be Shannon Conway's brother. For a minute. Sixty seconds.

"You bet!" Mr. Turner said, "I was coming to that."

"Well," Shannon said, "we would like some of those delicious greens in your garden!"

My ears almost fell off. So did Wilmer's and Harley's.

"Beet greens?" Mr. Turner smacked. "Shannon, you know what's good! Those greens are just right, and we have lots more than we can eat. Come on! I'll give you a bushel of them. It will be a good way to get them thinned."

So we took our aching backs right back to work. We had to pull out some little beets and leave some to grow. These were spaced about nine inches apart. The ones we pulled out were the greens.

We worked half an hour. Was I mad! Was I ashamed! My own brother. I could hardly believe the facts. I was very disgraced. Wilmer and Harley were disgusted.

Shannon did not notice. He looked happy, and I knew he was thinking about the best recipe to use.

Archibald seemed happy, too. "Mr. Turner," he said, "are you going to grow these beets to canning size?"

"Well," Mr. Turner said, "they will be that size, but this little garden is not for canning. There isn't a canning factory near enough."

71

"My father owns two canning factories," Archibald bragged. "He is looking for a place to build another."

Mr. Turner laughed. "Well, I could tell him a good place."

He meant Brookfield.

They were working on the same row, and they went on talking about canning factories.

I got a chance to speak a few words to Shannon. "Some brother!" I said. "Mr. Turner would have given us some chickens, but you had to ask for these old beet greens."

"We will have chicken on Kymie's birthday," Shannon said. "But we never have beet greens."

"Well, we have enough now," Wilmer said.

We had a basketful, and Mr. Turner said, "Hop in the car, men, and I'll run you home."

First he dropped Archibald at his house. "Thank you very much, sir," Archibald said, and he marched up the front walk with his armful of beet greens.

Shannon and I were last to get home. "Thanks again for the greens, Mr. Turner," Shannon said. "I'll cook them for supper just the way you said."

I said, "Mr. Turner, I wish to thank you for the dollar."

Toby wagged his tail very politely. Dogs eat chicken. They do not like beet greens.

I did not go into the house because I was too tired to clean the basement. Instead I went over to Wilmer's and we met Harley.

"Let's get something to eat," Wilmer said. "It will be beet greens or nothing tonight."

"That's right," Harley said. "My mother phoned my father at the office. I didn't know beet greens were so wonderful."

So we went to Vince's Drive-in and had some hamburgers with lots of dill pickles, and then we found some of the guys and played ball.

It was five o'clock when I went home. It was too late to clean the basement.

"Ma," I said, "I am very sorry to tell you that you have one dumb boy."

"Only one?" Ma said. "Hallelujah! When you have seven boys, you are doing very well if there is only one dumb one. Which is it?"

"It's Shannon," I said. "Mr. Turner would have given everybody a chicken, but Shannon had to go and ask for beet greens. I smell them cooking now. Are you cooking them?"

"Oh, no," Ma said. "I could never cook them to suit Shannon. He is cooking on the summer stove, and I am cooking chicken. Mr. Turner sent us some this afternoon. I believe Wilmer and Harley will be eating chicken, too."

Sure enough, we had chicken for supper. "Where is Shannon?" Pa said.

"Oh," Ma said, "Shannon is a little bit mad. He feels he is not appreciated. He is eating in the basement."

"Didn't he want some chicken?" Pa said.

"Chicken?" Ma said. "Chicken, when he tried out the perfect recipe for beet greens with side pork?"

Pa put down his fork very slowly and softly. He got a very strange look in his eyes. He said in a queer voice, "Did you say beet greens with side pork? And you're letting that poor little boy eat down in that dark, dank, cellar all alone, without the comfort and companionship of someone who loves him, beet greens and all?"

Pa stood. He looked as if he were dreaming, or about to walk in his sleep. "Excuse me," he said. He picked up his plate and fork and headed for the basement.

"Oh, Shannon isn't alone," Ma said. "He has a guest."

Something told me.

I went down to see.

Sure enough, Shannon's guest was Archibald Brewster. They were sitting at Ma's laundry table with their plates piled high with greens and meat, and they were stuffing their faces.

They grinned at Pa.

"Fellows," Pa said, "can you turn away a poor old man who has not tasted a beet green since he was a pale young drummer boy in the Revolution?"

Archibald said, "If you mean the American Revolution, sir, I believe that was from 1775 to 1781."

"That's almost two hundred years ago," Shannon said.

"Two hundred?" Pa said. "Well, it seems that long, fellows, since I had a dish of beet greens."

"Sit down, sir," Archibald said. "But we have a rule

here. Every man is allowed both elbows and one knee on the table, but no more. So don't try anything funny."

"Very good!" Pa said.

He passed his plate, and Shannon filled it with beet greens. Pa tasted and sighed a long sigh. "Excellent, Shannon, excellent! And I hear the hungry throngs descending!"

So all the family came down to eat beet greens in the basement, and after a while Archibald moaned. "Shannon," he said, "I am sorry to tell you that the greens are salty!"

"They sure are!" Pa said.

Then Baker came for Archibald, and I called up Wilmer.

"Wilmer," I said, "we cannot scare Archibald with Shannon's cooking. He likes it! He is full of it! Up to his ears!"

"Our long walk was wasted on Archibald, too," Wilmer said.

"Well, it was not wasted on me," I said. "If I had stayed home, Ma would have made me clean the basement. I would have had a hard, worky day."

It had not been a hard day, and Archibald was a good sport about a few things; but of course we could not let him spoil the big game.

CHAPTER VII

The Bumblebees Object

Archibald did not come to school Monday morning, and at recess Wilmer said, "Well, Ralph Jackson's seat was empty again this morning."

"Yes," Harley said. "I missed good old Ralph when we sang 'The Marines' Hymn.' And I noticed Archibald was absent, too. Maybe Nero bit him."

"Maybe Shannon's greens made him sick," Wilmer said.

"It was not Shannon's greens," I said. "And let's play ball. The big game is just two weeks from tomorrow."

The guys chose sides, and I batted first. It seemed very strange to see the bare spot on the sidewalk where Archibald always sat, to observe.

The game did not go very well. We did not hit very often, and Wilmer pitched wild. He pitched wild to Harley. Then he yelled, "Strike one!"

"Listen, Pitkin," Harley said. "That was a wild pitch, and you know it!"

"Strike one!" Wilmer yelled again.

Harley threw down the bat. "Pitkin," he said, "I am coming to show you!"

So Wilmer started to run, but Harley said, "Oh, I do not feel like chasing Pitkin around the school three times. I do not feel like playing ball today. I guess it is because I miss good old Ralph so much." He looked at the place where Archibald always sat.

Wilmer came and looked at it, too.

"I just had a good idea," I said. "When Archibald comes back, let's ask him to play ball in Ralph's place. Then we will not miss good old Ralph so much."

"Let's think about it a while," said Wilmer.

Archibald came back after the last recess. "Miss Kramer," he said "I have a note from my Aunt Grace. I had a slight toothache this morning and had to go to the dentist, but I have recovered."

Recovered.

Miss Kramer smiled at him. "I am certainly glad you are here, Archibald, because our class has something important to decide. Here is a letter from Miss Honeychurch and the Fifth Grade. Wanda, will you read it?"

Wanda walked up to the front, with her blue skirt

77

going swish and her two yellow pony tails flopping. She took the letter, turned around, and gave us a sweet smile which we did not care for. She took a deep breath and began to read at us.

"To the Sixth Grade: The Fifth Grade invites you to compete with us in a spelldown next Friday evening. We will invite our parents. There will be a prize for the best speller, and we will have a party afterward. R.S.V.P. The Fifth Grade."

I raised my hand. "Miss Kramer," I said, "I do not trust riddles. What does R.S.V.P. mean?"

Archibald raised his hand. "That is French for 'Answer, if you please,'" he said, and Glenora waggled those funny black eyelashes at him and sighed out loud.

Harley stood up. "Miss Kramer," he said, "I am an American. I am going to be a Marine. My ma and pa are Americans, and so are my brother and sisters. I do not trust people who have to write their letters in French. I like people who are not ashamed to say what they mean right out."

Wilmer stood up. "Miss Kramer," he said, "after some very deep thinking, I agree that this is a very dishonest-sounding letter. When you first hear it, you think it is about a party. But when you read between the lines, you find that it is very worky. I vote *no*."

"Well," Miss Kramer said, "everyone will now vote. How many are in favor of the spelldown?"

Some people raised their hands. "Fourteen," Miss

78

Kramer said. "How many are not in favor of the spell-down?"

The fellows raised their hands. "Thirteen," Miss Kramer said.

Wilmer stood up. "Miss Kramer," he said, "I demand a recount. I know there are fourteen fellows here, and every American boy would vote *no*. Of course, I do not know how a Frenchman would vote."

"I see," Miss Kramer said. "Wilmer, one boy voted in favor of the spelldown."

Sure enough, it was Archibald. He was sitting there dressed up, with a sweet smile on his face, voting the way good old Ralph would never have voted. All the girls were giving him very disgusting smiles because he was voting with them.

"O. K.," Wilmer said. "I guess there are only thirteen real guys and one Frenchman, after all."

"A fine thing!" Harley said, after school. "We have got to stand up on our tired feet and be spelled down by the Fifth Grade and disgrace our mothers, because good old Ralph moved away."

Well, I thought, my brother Shannon is the best speller in the Fifth Grade so maybe my mother will not be so disgraced.

But I said, "You're right, Harley. Ralph would not be caught dead voting for a spelldown."

"Very true," Wilmer said. "Ralph was against spell-downs and tests and homework. Ralph was against people who write their dishonest, worky notes in French. Ralph always wrote English."

"Miss Kramer didn't say so," Wonderful Wanda said. "Miss Kramer said Ralph's writing looked like a foreign language sometimes."

We were not talking to the girls.

"I miss Ralph," Wilmer said. "And I have changed our minds. We will not invite Archibald to take Ralph's place on the Brookfield Bumblebees' team."

"Let's go tell him," I said. "Let's go right over to his house and tell him that he will have to play catch with the girls." I gave the girls one of my smiles but not the sweet kind. "Do you girls wish to come along?" I said. "We are taking the shortcut."

"No, thank you!" said Gorgeous Glenora.

"Well, you did when we were in the Fourth Grade," Harley said. "Wanda, you could waggle across a garage roof faster than we could."

"That was only because I have manners," Wanda said. "That was only so that my shoes would not break the roof."

Well, that is why we waggle, too.

We ran away and left the girls standing there. We ran down the alley between Oak Street and Caroline. We cut across the corner lot to Dennis Place. We ran into Wilmer's Aunt Harriet's yard and climbed her fence and crawled up on her garage. We flopped down on our stomachs and wiggle-waggled across the garage roof to the other edge. Then we crawled into the tree, and we could see Archibald's yard, with Archibald in it.

Our ears almost fell off.

Archibald was playing ball. He had a brand new ball and bat. He would throw the ball above his head and try to bat it. Sometimes he hit it, zing! He tried to hit it against the garage so that it would bounce back to him. Sometimes he did not hit it at all.

Once when he missed it, he yelled something that sounded like "Wild pitch!"

Wilmer yelled, too. Wilmer couldn't help it. "That was a strike!" Wilmer yelled.

He clapped his hands over his mouth, but Archibald heard him. He stopped batting and came down to the back of the yard.

"What are you doing up there?" he yelled.

"We came to tell you something," I said.

"About baseball," Wilmer said.

"Then come down here!" Archibald yelled.

So we went down to the gate, and Archibald let us in. He put his bat in my hands. "This is my new bat, Trent," he said. "How do you like it?"

"How can I tell?" I said. "I never batted with it."

"Bat with it now," Archibald said. "I will pitch."

He ran back and sent the ball at me, and I hit at it and missed.

"Wild pitch!" Wilmer yelled.

The ball rolled over close to Nero. Nero growled.

"Wait a minute!" Archibald said. "Nero sounds nervous." He came and looked at the ball. Nero growled and showed those big teeth. Then he began to jump in the air and pull his chain and bark.

Baker came out of the house. "Archibald," he said, "your aunt wishes to invite your friends to tea. I will get the ball."

Tea. We had forgotten about tea. It would not be tea. It would be goat's milk and wafers.

Harley and Wilmer looked pale. I felt pale, myself.

"Come on!" Archibald said.

"Well, Archibald," I said, "it is too bad to waste good, expensive goat's milk on us. I mean, we are used to common cow's milk in bottles."

"Yes," Wilmer said. "If you will excuse us, we will just shinny up the tree."

But something happened. Archibald's Aunt Grace came out. She was a tall lady with white hair and black earrings and a purple and white dress.

"Aunt Grace," Archibald said, "may I introduce my friends. Trenton Conway, Harley Scott, and Wilmer Pitkin. This is my aunt, Mrs. Cleveland, boys."

We have manners. We smiled, if it killed us, and we said how-do-you-do to Archibald's father's Aunt Grace.

"Do come in," she said. "I saw you playing ball, so Hazel has your tea ready."

"Mrs. Cleveland," I said, "it would be too bad to drink up all your goat's milk."

"Oh, Archibald has told me that you don't like goat's milk," Mrs. Cleveland said. "Your tea will be chocolate cake and cocoa. Archibald, dear show them the guest towels."

We washed up, but we all used the same towel.

Then we had tea. It was not getting dark, but there were candles on the table. Everyone had a piece of cake on a plate, with a little fork. The cocoa was very good. There were little napkins with some lace on them. But our pants were not exactly clean, so we did not spoil the napkins.

"How is your baseball team doing?" Mrs. Cleveland asked.

"Keen," said Wilmer. He was trying to make some cake stay on his little fork.

"Let me see," she said. "I believe Archibald says you call yourselves the Bumblebees."

"Right!" said Harley.

She smiled. "I suppose you have little bees on your uniforms. Archibald, dear, why don't you bring your uniform home to be washed?"

I almost swallowed my little fork. Archibald's aunt thought he was a Bumblebee. She thought we had uniforms.

"We do not have uniforms," I said.

She looked surprised. "Why in the world don't you?"

"Well," Wilmer said, "it is because there is not enough money in Brookfield."

"That's right," Harley said. "Brookfield does not grow. My dad says that when the boys grow up, they move to some other town and some girls find them and chase after them until they catch them and get married to them. Then it's the grindstone, brother, the grindstone! That means they have to work so hard to earn a living for their wives that they never come back to Brookfield and the dear scenes of their boyhood." Harley felt of his lip. "So I am raising a black mustache to scare the girls away."

"Let me see," said Mrs. Cleveland. She looked at Harley's lip. "Yes," she said, "I think I can see it coming."

Well, it was a little chocolate frosting, but we were too polite to say so and break old Harley's heart.

"Mrs. Cleveland," I said, "there are not enough mills and factories and jobs in Brookfield. My dad says that what Brookfield needs is a few good factories."

"I believe it does," said Archibald's aunt. "I believe it does."

Well, we thanked her for the cake and cocoa, and she took us to the front door. So we had to walk home on the sidewalk.

"How do you like that?" Wilmer said. "She thinks Archibald is on our team."

"Look, Wilmer," I said. "I've got news for you. When Archibald pitched to me, it was not a wild pitch. If it had been a game, and if Archibald had pitched as well as he can wrestle and hike, and if it had been my off-day, he might have struck me out!"

"Too many 'if's,'" Wilmer said. "Anyway, Archibald voted with the girls. Trent, I hope you will not have him pestering around your house anymore setting a bad example for the twins."

"Can I help it if he comes?" I said.

"Well," Wilmer said, "I do not think he would ever go back to your house if you made him help clean the basement."

I moaned a little. "Ma has not mentioned the basement for a few days. Don't bring that up!"

"Mothers and elephants never forget," Wilmer said.

"I think there will be a big blow-up at your house any night."

"Worry, worry!" I said. "I have too much to worry about: the basement, the big game, and Archibald!"

"Don't forget the spelldown," Harley said.

Well, when I got home, I got the bad news. Shannon had to go home and tell Ma about the spelldown.

"Trenton," Ma said, "you and Shannon may drill each other in spelling every night after supper so that you both know every word in the book and do not disgrace me on Friday night."

So after supper we had to spell. Hank and Kymie pronounced the words.

"Miss Honeychurch says I am a naturally good speller," Shannon bragged.

I said, "Miss Honeychurch, Miss Honeychurch, Miss Honeychurch. It is going to break your heart if you get spelled down before Miss Honeychurch, isn't it?"

"You keep out of it," Shannon said. "Next word, Kymie."

The word was *unbelievable*. Shannon spelled it wrong.

"That is a sticker for me," he said. "I hope I don't get that one Friday night. I'm afraid I'll get nervous and spell it wrong."

"You will learn it," I said. "We have to practice spelling tomorrow night and Wednesday night and Thursday night, too. And it's all Archibald's fault."

CHAPTER VIII

A Clothes Chute Rescue

On Tuesday Archibald tried to walk home from school with me. "Where is Baker?" I said.

"Oh," Archibald said, "my aunt had something for Baker to do. She told me he would not pick me up."

He kept walking.

It took me quite a while to get home. I went around past Wilmer's house, but I did not go in because I could see Wilmer's mother hiding behind the curtain with a broom in her hand.

"Wilmer," I said, "you will have to think fast to think yourself out of sweeping the garage."

Wilmer said, "I think I will go home with you, Trent. We will bat a few."

But just then his door opened, and his mother said a few words, and Wilmer decided to stay home.

Next, we walked toward Harley's house, and we could see a lady pushing a baby buggy up and down, very slowly, on the front walk.

"Your mother seems to be looking for someone, Harley," I said.

"I think I will go home with you, Trent," Harley said. "We will bat a few."

"Harley Scott," his mother said, "I told you to be here at four o'clock!"

"I have changed my mind, Trent," Harley said. "I think I will offer to push my little sister around the block and save Ma the trouble."

"And save yourself some!" his mother said.

Well, I knew Archibald did not have a baby sister, and he could not sweep his garage, because that is a dirty job for a boy who has to keep his hands and best clothes clean. So I said, "Archibald, I will show you a shortcut home."

"Oh, Wilmer showed me," Archibald said. "But it is not a shortcut. It is too crooked. Baker says a straight line is the shortest distance between two points. I will go home with you. We can bat a few."

Well, I should have known it was coming, but I shook, a little.

We went to my house, but before I went inside, Ma was yelling at me. "Trent Conway, darling, I want you

88

boys to get that basement swept! And swept before supper!"

Well, I did not want to bat with Archibald, but I did not want to clean the basement either.

"Come along, Archibald," I said.

I went to the kitchen to see how mad Ma looked. She was making cookies, and Shannon was washing some fish in the sink.

Ma gave Archibald a very sweet smile. "Sit down, Archibald," she said. "Won't you have some cookies?"

She gave me a different look. "Before supper, Trent," she said.

"But, Ma," I said, "it's not polite to go and have a lot of fun cleaning up the basement when I have company."

"I would love to have Archibald for company," Ma said. She gave him another smile, and a plate of cookies, and a napkin.

I sat down beside the cookies that were cooling.

"Ma," I said, "do you want us to break our backs and die?"

"Not particularly," she said. "I never heard of anyone dying from sweeping out a basement."

"Look, Mom," I said. "Most accidents are in homes, right? Many are on the stairs, right? Our basement stairs are very steep, right? Well, where is the broom?"

"It's in the broom closet," Ma said.

"Well, someone has to walk across the waxed floor and open the broom closet and carry the broom down the stairs to the basement. Hanky would probably fall and break his back and suffer many years on a bed of pain. Where is our dustpan?"

"It's in the broom closet," Ma said.

"Well, someone has to walk across the waxed floor and open the broom closet and carry the dustpan down the stairs to the basement. Poor little Corky would probably break his poor little back on that job. I can shut my eyes and see him bleeding and dying and trudging on, because you want the basement cleaned. Where is our trash can?"

"It's out beside the garage," Ma said.

"Well, someone has to walk across this waxed floor and go down the back steps and walk down the drive, where all the delivery trucks come, and pick up the trash can and carry it bumpety-bump down the drive and down the steep basement stairs. Joel would probably fall and break his spine and die on the job."

"Don't make it Kymie," Shannon said. "Kymie will be needed around here. I can see that he won't have to give funerals for crickets for three or four days."

"This is serious," I said. "Mom, sweeping the basement is a job that is very hard on the heart. Dad said so the day he swept it and then watched the last game of the world series. I am your oldest. I am your pride and joy. Trenton J. Conway, Junior. So I would do the sweeping, and I would probably swoon and die with the last feeble swipe of the broom."

Ma said, "You break my heart, darling."

"Well, then," I said, "someone would have to carry the broom and dustpan up to the closet again. It would probably be the last twin you have that can wiggle, Jerry."

"Trent, honey, have another cooky," Mom said. "You've been through a lot. You need it. You've had only seven."

"Thanks, Ma," I said. "Well, then Shannon would have to carry the trash can up from the basement, bumpety-bump, bumpety-bump, banging his shinny bones black and blue."

"Shin bones," said Archibald.

"Shin bones," I said. "Well, if Shannon got to the top alive, Sensenbrenner's deliver man would run him down without mercy and back up to see what he had run over."

"Hold it!" Ma wiped her eyes. "With my last feeble breath, I will walk across this waxed floor and turn off the oven," she said.

"What's the matter, Ma?" I asked. "You can't turn off the oven."

"Oh, can't I? The cookies are done, and Dad and I won't need eighteen baked potatoes and all those stuffed chops. Bread and butter will do for us at our lonely board."

Lonely board. She meant the table.

"But, Ma!" I said. "We aren't dead, yet. If we don't clean the basement, there is hope!"

91

"Darling, dead or alive, you aren't coming to the table unless the basement is cleaned," Ma said.

I went over to look at Shannon's fish.

"Don't look at me!" Shannon said. "There's only enough for me."

"What is it?" I said.

"It's fish."

"What kind of fish?"

"Turtle," said Shannon.

"No, thanks!" I said, "Did it get past Ma?"

"You bet!"

Just then I heard a clatter. It was the Lightning Express being sent down by Hank and Kymie for cookies.

"No more cookies B.B.," Ma said, meaning "Before Basement."

I tore a scrap off Ma's want book and wrote a note.

You guys swep the basement, or else. Ma.

I put the note in the coffee can and sent it up. Then I got the broom and dustpan and carried them up to Joel and Jerry's room. Archibald tagged along.

Joel and Jerry were watching a TV program on the set they had bought for fifteen dollars. They had their heads together and looked just alike, with their new haircuts and black eyes.

"Down the chute, men!" I said. "We have to clean the basement."

So the twins slid down the clothes chute, and I dropped the broom and dustpan after them.

Then I went over to Hank and Kymie's room. They were working on the Diesel that they were painting on their wall. Hank was painting, and Kymie was standing back advising him. Even though they do not look exactly alike because one of them is adopted, Pa says they are twins under their skin. As I walked into the room, I knew what Pa meant. The look on their faces was just exactly the same.

"You still here?" I said. "You got Ma's note, didn't you?"

"We recognized your fingerprints," Hanky said. "Also your spelling."

Kymie said, "You'd better look out or the Fifth Grade will beat you Friday night. And since when are you Ma's secretary?"

"Ma means business," I said. "No clean basement, no supper."

So we climbed out the front window and duck-walked down the porch roof and slid down the porch post to the ground. Archibald stood in the window watching us.

"Come on!" I yelled. "Ralph always came down this way."

Archibald smiled. He said, "Perhaps good old Ralph had not heard that a straight line is the shortest distance between two points. I shall see you."

I brought the trash can from the garage and took it to the basement window. Joel and Jerry opened the window for us. We slid in, can and all, and in a minute Shannon slid in, too.

"Where is Archibald?" Shannon said. "Did he go?"

Just then we heard two noises. One was on the kitchen floor. Ma was tapping and calling, "Baker is waiting out front for Archibald, darlings!"

The other noise was Archibald, yelling. "Trent! Trent! How do I get out of here?"

I took one look, and then I crawled out the window and ran down the driveway to Archibald's car.

Baker opened the door. He said, "Archibald's aunt wishes him to come home to tea."

"Well," I said, "I am very sorry. Archibald can not come right now because he is stuck in the clothes chute."

"The clothes chute!" Baker scrambled out of the car. "What are you doing about it?" he said. "Call someone! Call the fire department! This is terrible!"

"But," I said, "Archibald isn't on fire. He is just cuddled up in the chute like a squirrel. Pa will get him out."

"When is your father coming home?" Baker asked.

"Well," I said, "it might be eleven o'clock. He might be having supper with some other lawyers and businessmen. They are going to discuss ways to make Brookfield grow so that there will be more business."

"Eleven o'clock!" Baker said. "Boy, this is an emergency! I shall have to get aid, if your mother will permit."

"Oh, Ma's always glad to have people pulled out of the clothes chute before supper," I said.

94

Just then Pa's station wagon turned into the driveway. Baker went over to talk.

"Mr. Conway," he said, "Archibald Brewster is imprisoned in your clothes chute."

"Arch?" Pa said. "In the clothes chute? In his good clothes?" Pa laughed so hard that I laughed, too.

Baker waited until we were through laughing. "I am very sorry to trouble you," he said.

"Oh, it's no trouble at all, Mr. Baker," Pa said. "This isn't bath night. We won't need the chute. We'll get Archibald out after awhile."

"Will you please hurry?" Baker said. "Archibald's tea is waiting."

"Oh, in that case," Pa said, "there is no time to lose. Mr. Baker, you are invited to the daring rescue. We'll put a hackamore on Archibald."

"A hackamore!" Baker said. "Mr. Conway, do you know what a hackamore is?"

"I do," I said, "It is something they use to train horses. But this is different. I'll get the rope, Pa."

I brought the rope from the garage, and we went upstairs to the twins' room. Pa called down the clothes chute so loud that the house shook.

"Hello! Hello below there! Archibald Brewster, if you can hear me, make some feeble sign!"

Archibald waved one hand a little. "I can hear you," he said.

"So can I, darling!" Ma yelled.

95

Pa was being funny because Archibald was looking right up into his face.

"How are your teeth?" Pa said. "You are supposed to grip this hackamore in them for your daring rescue."

"I can't do that, Mr. Conway," Archibald said. "But maybe I can whinny a little."

It was a joke. Pa and I laughed and Archibald giggled a little, and Baker said, "Rather clever!"

Then Pa said, "Well, this will be just a wash day or boiled potato type of rescue, after all. Here's the rope, Archibald. Get a good, firm grip with your paws. Got it? Hang on! Alley-oop! Here we are!"

Archibald came up smiling. "Thank you!" he said.

"Any time!" Pa said. "And I am glad to see that you have the old spirit of 1492. Columbus, also, took a chance. Do you wish to make a statement?"

Baker said, "How in the world did this happen?"

"Well," Archibald said, "you are to blame, Baker. You told me that a straight line is the shortest distance between two points. I thought the chute was a straight line to the basement, but I found out that it curves a little and gets narrow."

"That's right," I said. "The twins can still get through, but all the rest of us have been stuck."

Kymie yelled from the basement. "Hey, Trent! Let's get some action!"

"Baker," Archibald said, "it is my duty to help clean the basement."

"Oh, that's all right," I said. "You can't clean the basement in those clothes, Archibald."

So Archibald went home, and we cleaned the basement, and nobody got his back broken.

When we finished, Dad came to inspect. "Well, you hit all the high spots, gentlemen," he said. "Your old man will carry that can upstairs. You scram and get ready for supper."

So we went upstairs, and Ma said, "How did you ever get the basement cleaned so fast? Or did the brownies do it?"

"Oh, we did it just the way we always do," I said.

"Risking our lives." I rubbed my back a little and stooped over as I walked.

"Well, get ready for supper," Ma said. "Corky is all washed up. And after supper you will have to do some spelling. Remember?"

I told the guys about it Wednesday morning. "Cleaning the basement will not keep Archibald away," I said. "We might as well face it. He came up out of the clothes chute smiling. And he is beginning to hint about batting a few."

Wilmer shook his head. "A guy who would vote for a spelldown cannot play ball," he said. "I wish Archibald would forget it and stick to his spelling. I will have to think this out."

CHAPTER IX

A Game of Hide-and-seek

On Wednesday night there was another big blow-up around our house. It was because of Ma's good bracelet box.

It started this way. Right after school, I found Archibald sitting on our front porch.

I was very polite. I said, "Hello, Archibald. How is your aunt? I imagine she will be sending Baker for you soon for tea."

Before Archibald could say *yes* or *no*, Kymie slid down the porch post with the sad news.

"What is that in your hand?" I asked him.

"Well," he said, "I am giving a funeral."

"You can't," I said. "All the mice that lived in Mrs.

99

Miller's mop closet have had funerals. The baby robin that fell out of the nest is buried. You even gave a funeral for a cricket. There is nothing left around Oak Street to bury."

"O.K., Trenton, if that's what you think," Kymie said, "you just come to the funeral! Joel and Jerry are sliding down the clothes chute right now, to be in the parade. I have dug the grave."

He walked away, and I looked at Archibald. He was staring after Kymie, with both hands in his pockets.

I am not as great a thinker as Wilmer Pitkin, but I did think that maybe Archibald would not bother around my house any more if he went to this funeral.

"Come on, Archibald," I said. "When Kymie gives a funeral, it is our duty to go. If you do not care to shed

a few tears for the deceased, you may just observe."

Archibald looked down the street, but Baker was not coming in the long car.

We went to the back yard. Hanky was there with his harmonica, playing a very sad tune. Then Joel and Jerry came out of the garage carrying a little white box, and they sang a very sad song that Grandpa sings to us. It is called "In the Sweet By-and-by."

Then Kymie came out in Pa's long black coat.

We all marched very slowly to Kymie's burying ground. Kymie put the little box in the grave and put some dirt and grass over it.

"Rest in peace," he said. "Ladies and gentlemen, the twins will now sing a song at you."

So the twins sang:

"Swing low, sweet chariot,
Coming for to carry me home,
Swi-ing low, sweet chariot,
Coming for to carry me home!"

While they sang, Hanky tootled very softly on the harmonica, and Toby sat on his tail and cried because the music hurt his ears.

Shannon came down the drive and yelled: "Hey, cut the racket! Mrs. Miller says she can't hear herself at the telephone!"

So the funeral was over, and Archibald took his hands out of his pockets.

"Very sad," I said.

"Indeed," said Archibald. "What died?"

"Shannon wouldn't tell us," I said. "A bee, maybe. Archibald, I guess your Aunt Grace will be sending Baker after you. It's almost supper time."

But Ma came out on the porch and smiled at Archibald. "Wouldn't you like to stay to supper?" she said. "We're having beef roast."

"Thank you," Archibald said. "I should love to stay." He went in the house to telephone his aunt.

"Well, how do you like that?" I said to Kymie. "I thought the guy would run home because he does not like funerals, and now he is staying here to supper."

At supper time Archibald said, "Mrs. Conway, I will wash when Trent does, and use his towel like good old Ralph."

Ma looked a little surprised, but she said. "That will be nice, Archibald."

So when it was my turn, we went up and washed and slopped the soap around and sloshed the towel around. Of course, Archibald was not Ralph, but I could shut my eyes and almost think it was good old Ralph pulling the other end of the towel.

Archibald helped wipe up the washbowl and push the bathroom rug over a few soapsuds, and we wiped our hands on our pants some more and went down, and Archibald forgot to comb his hair.

Supper was ready. After grace, Pa said, "Supper! Supper! All pitch in, for Old Dan Tucker!"

"Oh, Daddy!" Ma said. "Really! Shouldn't you learn a new poem?"

"No," Pa said. "That's my trusty poem. I believe in learning one poem and sticking to it." He fixed a big plate for Archibald. "I want to see every smitch of this disappear," he said. "I've been feeding you for eleven years, more or less, and I like to see a little fat on my kids' bones."

Joel giggled. "Pa, that is not your kid."

"Any kid that soaks my soap and parks his feet under my table is my kid," Pa said. He gave Corky a plate.

Ma looked at Corky, too. She seemed to remember something, and that was when we had this very big blow-up.

"Corky, darling," Ma said, "did you take anything to

school today? Anything made of white plastic and lined with silk?"

"Not me!" said Corky. "All I tooked was my teddy bear."

"Shannon," Ma said, "darling, did you make a gift to some beautiful, sweet, wonderful, charming, completely perfect person who is overworked and underpaid by the school board?"

She meant his teacher, and Shannon turned as red as his hair because he had this terrible case on Miss Honeychurch.

"We will open the defense," Pa said. "Careful, Shannon! Anything you say may be used against you."

Shannon said, "Ma, if you mean did I take your bracelet box to Miss Honeychurch, you just leave her out of this!"

Pa moaned. "I warned the boy!"

"Ma," Shannon said, "you'd better look at Kymie. Mr. Kymie gave a very fancy funeral today."

"Kymie, darling," Ma said, "have you seen my bracelet box?"

"Yes, ma'am," said Kymie. He looked cross-eyed at his nose and tried to lick some gravy off it. "Many times, ma'am."

Well, when Kymie is that polite, you know he is guilty.

"Philetus, darling, where did you last see it?" Ma asked.

Philetus is Kymie's real name; and when Ma calls him that, things are bad.

"Well," Kymie gulped. He looked up at the ceiling. "Well," he said, "two little boys were bearing it sadly away. Their sad little eyes were lifted on high, and their sad little voices were lifted in a sad, sad song." When Kymie is guilty, he pretends he does not care. He sang a little.

"In the sweet by-and-by . . ."

"I am touched," Ma said. "Where did the sad little boys bear the box?"

"Well," Kymie said, "they bore it to yonder burying ground, and I placed it gently in the earth." He was still pretending.

"That's right, Ma," said Joel and Jerry.

Corky was watching Kymie. Corky's eyes were big and round and full of tears.

"May I ask," Pa said, "who departed this vale of tears?"

"Well, Pa," Hanky said, "you know the bat that lived back of the garage door? He departed."

"May he rest in peace," Kymie said. He stopped pretending. "Look, Ma. I thought you said that box was junk. Honest! I thought that was the one, Ma. I'll pay for it!"

Right then Corky opened his mouth very wide and began to howl. Joel and Jerry looked as if they would cry, too.

"Come, come!" Ma said. "I didn't know you were so in love with the bat. I have seen you after him with a broom many times. Don't cry, darlings. It's all right. Kymie gave the bat a nice funeral and put him in my bracelet box. And now maybe if we all smile and eat our supper we will get another bat. And maybe I'll get another jewelry box."

"You bet you will, Duchess!" Pa said. "I'm so glad to get rid of—Excuse me!" Pa looked sad. "I mean, of course, we must all bear up. Bear up, Corky!"

So we had chocolate cake, and Pa said, "Mother, which boy is our guest? Under the chocolate frosting they all look alike to me."

Shannon poked Archibald. Then Shannon said. "I am the guest. Mrs. Conway, the cake is delicious. I imagine you made it with your own lily hands. In case you are offering seconds to guests—"

"Guests and everybody else, while it lasts!" Ma said.

So we had seconds, and Corky ate his and began to howl again. "Ow-oo! Ow-oo!"

"Come, man!" Pa said. "Forget the bat."

"I forgot the bat," Corky said. "But I tooked my teddy bear to school, and I lefted him there! Ow-oo! Ow-oo!"

"Oh, dear!" Ma said. "And the school is locked. Corky, darling, Teddy will be all right."

Just then Baker sounded the horn, and Archibald had to go. He backed out, thanking and thanking, and we watched him ride away, while Corky howled.

"My goodness!" Ma said. "I know Archibald never saw such a house!"

"Well, goody!" I said. "Maybe he will stop being around, and I can get some batting done."

After supper Shannon and I had to study spelling. Kymie pronounced the words. Joel and Jerry and Hanky spelled, too; and when Shannon missed *unbelievable*, Hanky spelled it right.

Corky watched TV and cried, and Ma popped a big bowl of popcorn.

Corky ate popcorn and cried, and Pa said, "I will take you on for a game of checkers, Corky." So they played two games, and Corky won both.

"There!" Pa said. He looked at the clock and began to howl about bedtime.

"I want Teddy! I won't go to bed without Teddy!" screeched Corky.

Right then the doorbell rang, and who should be standing there but Archibald?

"Good evening, Mrs. Conway," he said. "I just thought I'd drop by."

"Oh, come in, Archibald!" Ma said. "Corky, Corky! See what Archibald has brought! Your Teddy!"

Sure enough, Archibald walked in with Corky's teddy bear. Corky grabbed it and hugged it, and Ma said, "How did you do it, Archibald?"

"It was quite simple," Archibald said. "I had Aunt Grace find out who is on the school board. Baker and I borrowed a key to the school."

"You are a very kind, thoughtful boy," Ma said.

"Won't you sit down for a little while, Archibald?"

Archibald sat down and smiled at all of us. He was a hero.

"Next case!" Pa yelled. He pointed. "Up those stairs! You, and you, and you!"

Corky and Joel and Jerry went up. Archibald watched TV and ate popcorn with us.

After a while Pa pointed at Hanky and Kymie and yelled, "Up those stairs! You and you!"

We heard Joel yelling upstairs. "Hurry up, you guys! We want to play hide-and-seek!"

"Well, Archibald," I said, "I guess Shannon and I will be next."

"Are you going to play hide-and-seek?" Archibald asked.

"It's only make-believe," Shannon told him.

Archibald stayed until Pa looked at the clock and pointed to Shannon and me. "Up those stairs! You and you!"

I looked at Archibald. I am very polite to company. "Come upstairs and play hide-and-seek a few minutes until you go home," I said.

"Thank you," said Archibald.

We went upstairs, and Shannon and I hustled into our pajamas. Then Shannon went into the twins' room.

"Where's Toby?" he said. "This is my night. Come on! Which of you guys has him?"

"Joel," Jerry said.

"Jerry," Joel said, but he giggled.

Shannon gave Joel's covers a yank, and there was Toby, all hunched up, waiting. Shannon grabbed him up, came back, tossed him into his bed, and hopped in with him.

I jumped into my bed. "Sit by the window, Archibald," I said, "so you can see Baker when he comes."

"O.K., gang!" Kymie yelled. "Let's play hide-and-seek before Corky goes to sleep!"

Corky was sleeping with Kymie. It was Corky's turn to hide first.

"I'm hided!" he yelled.

"Possible or impossible?" Shannon yelled.

"I can do it!" Corky said.

Shannon guessed. "Under the sofa?"

"No!"

I guessed. "In the broom closet?"

"No!"

"In the garage?" Joel guessed.

"NO! No! No!" Corky laughed.

We knew where he was all the time, but we guessed every place.

At last Kymie guessed. "In the clothes chute?"

Corky began to howl. "You peeked! You peeked!"

"Aw, I didn't!" Kymie said. It was his turn.

"Possible or impossible?" we yelled.

"Impossible!"

Joel guessed. "The Lightning Express!"

"No!"

Hanky guessed. "The cooky jar!"

"No!"

Archibald guessed. "Are you in the mailbox?"

"Come again!"

We guessed until Joel and Jerry and Corky quit guessing, and we knew they were asleep.

"Give up?" Kymie said.

Everyone gave up.

"I'm in the Diesel!" Kymie yelled. "Toot! Toot! Toot!"

"Hey, that's not fair!" Shannon said. "That Diesel is only painted on your wall. It's impossible to get in it."

"I said it was impossible!" Kymie said.

"He sure did!" said Archibald. "Toot! Toot! Toot!"

"O.K.," Shannon said. "O.K.! You get another turn."

But Ma yelled upstairs. "Archibald, dear, Mr. Baker is waiting!"

Archibald said good night and went down, and Shannon said, "Baker was out there all the time!"

"Well," I said, "why didn't you say so?"

"Oh," Shannon said, "Archibald looked kind of lonesome."

"Well," I said, "he is a hero tonight because he brought the bear, and I guess he will want to be on the team. Wilmer will be very mad!"

CHAPTER X

Everyone Participates

On Thursday we counted days, and Wilmer said, "The big game is one week from Tuesday. We will have to do some better pitching and batting and catching."

"Right," said Harley. "My cousin goes to school in Lawson. He says their best batter can bat a ball into the sky, and Victor Valley can pitch a shut-out. My cousin says we will have to go some to beat the Lawson Lions this year."

"O.K.," I said, "less talk and more action!"

"First batter!" Harley said.

Just then we saw Archibald coming.

"Wait a minute," I said, "Here comes Archibald. Archibald, I suppose you are going to observe."

"I feel I have observed almost long enough," Archibald said. He did not have a ball, but he pretended to wind up and pitch. "I feel I am about ready to participate in the game."

Participate.

Wilmer moaned a terrible moan. But before he could think of anything to say, Archibald was talking again.

"However," Archibald said, "first things first. The spelldown is tomorrow evening. I have a suggestion. I think we should spend recess practicing spelling."

This was the most horrible idea we ever heard. It was bad enough to have to practice spelling at home every night. But Wanda and Glenora and Susie and the girls agreed with Archibald.

"The Sixth Grade has never been beaten by the Fifth Grade," Wanda said. "But I have heard that four of the Fifth Grade boys and all the Fifth Grade girls get one hundred in spelling every day."

Well, Archibald was the only Sixth Grade boy who got one hundred every day, although sometimes the rest of us got one hundred.

"We are going down to the corner of the playground to have a spelldown," Susie said. "Wanda will pronounce the words. Every loyal Sixth Grader will come."

"I am a loyal Sixth Grader," I said, "but I will not come. The game with the Lawson Lions is only twelve days away!"

"Which is more important in life," Wanda asked, "to be

a good speller or to be a good baseball player? You just ask Miss Kramer!"

"Well," I said, "you just ask the Lawson Lions." Then I had a better idea. "Ask Archibald!" I said.

So Archibald had his chance, and what did he say?

"Both are important," he said, "but the spelldown is coming first."

Wilmer thought of something. "Archibald," he said, "we need good baseball players, but we need good spellers, too. So we are going to be big about this. We will not be mad if you go and practice spelling instead of baseball."

"A fine idea!" I said. "I am sure good old Ralph would feel that we were doing the right thing."

So Archibald went with the girls.

Harley batted first, and Wilmer pitched. "Strike one!" Wilmer yelled.

"That was not a strike!" Harley said. "That was a ball, and you know it."

"You swung," Wilmer said. He sent the ball again. "Strike two!" he yelled.

"That was a ball!" Harley said.

"Strike two!" Wilmer yelled again. He wound up and sent the ball. It was only a ball. "Strike three!" he yelled. "You're out!"

Harley showed all his teeth, and it was not a smile. "I'll show you!" Harley yelled. And then we saw Miss Kramer coming with thirteen girls and Archibald.

"Boys!" Miss Kramer said. "Wilmer. Trenton. All of you. Harley. Come here. Wanda had a perfectly wonderful idea, and I am disappointed that you turned it down. Wanda thinks you should spend recesses practicing spelling, and so do I. Come on. Line up!"

So that was the horrible way we had to spend recess, and we knew it was Archibald's idea.

At noon I said, "I do not think I care to speak to Sixth Graders who are not loyal to the Sixth Grade. That goes for all the girls."

"It goes for Archibald, too," Wilmer said. "After this, we will make no reply to remarks made by those persons."

So we had a spelldown during every recess Thursday and Friday. But we did not speak to the girls and Archibald.

"Miss Kramer," Wanda said, "the boys will not speak to us."

Miss Kramer smiled. "Well, that's just fine. You may write anything you wish to say, and they may reply in writing. And since I am a girl, they may write to me, too, and they had better spell all the words right."

So we had to write every single thing we wanted to say to Miss Kramer. We had to write, "May I sharpen a pencil?" and "May I get a library book?"

I wrote, "*I forgot my gimnasium shoes. May I borrow my brother's?*"

Miss Kramer would not answer me, and I had to look

up "*gymnasium*" and then write it ten times. I had never done so much writing before, and neither had the other fellows.

Archibald wrote me a note which I did not answer. He wrote: "*Dear Trent: Don't be angry at me. When the spelldown is over, I shall be glad to participate in the ball game. This may sound unbelievable, but I can bat straight and hard, and I can pitch a curve or a straight ball. We will beat Lawson. Yea!*"

Participate.

The girls kept writing notes to us, too. Wanda drew some hearts on her note to me. She wrote, "*Trent, aren't you sorry you were so stuborn?*"

That did not look right to me. So I looked up "*stubborn*," and I found that Wanda did not know how to spell it.

I wrote her a note. "*Please learn to spell before you write to me and before you participate in the spelldown.*" I did not put any hearts on it.

But Wanda drew some hearts on it and put it in her pocket.

The spelldown was in the gym on Friday night. The Fifth Grade was lined up on one side, and the Sixth Grade on the other. All the parents were sitting between us.

Miss Kramer and Miss Honeychurch were up in front, dressed up and smiling and smiling. Miss Remington, the Fourth Grade teacher, pronounced the words.

115

Poor old Wilmer had bad luck. He was the very first guy to be spelled down. His word was *horizon,* and he spelled it: *h-o-r-i-z-z-o-n.* When he sat down, he grinned at me and whispered, "Wild pitch!"

Next Miss Honeychurch's smartest girl, Priscilla Trask, had very bad luck. Her word was *dictionary* and she spelled it: *d-i-c-t-i-o-n-e-r-y.*

Then she had to go and cry. "I got nervous!" she said. "I know how to spell it! I just got nervous!"

But nerves do not count in a spelldown.

The next one down was Harley's dear, dear cousin, Susie Scott. Susie cried, too. She said she did not hear the word very well. But that did not count. She was out.

Some more Fifth Graders went down, and then Harley put two *b*'s in *neighbor.*

Gorgeous Glenora was looking at Harley through her eyelashes, and that was why she went down. She spelled *going* with a *w*, *g-o-w-i-n-g.* She really did know better.

Shannon spelled it right, and soon there were only four Sixth Graders and four Fifth Graders left.

The next hard word was *disappoint,* and that was Wanda's bad luck. She had on a yellow dress and had yellow bows in her hair, and when she sat down she kind of flipped her skirt and winked fast, but she did not cry.

The next hard word was *patient,* and soon only Shannon and Archibald and I were left.

Archibald spelled *judgment.* Shannon spelled *weird.*

116

Wilmer moaned. "This could go on all night!" We could smell coffee and see two ladies cutting pies in the kitchen.

I spelled *happily* and Archibald spelled *desperate*.

Archibald's Aunt Grace was smiling at Archibald. Ma and Pa were smiling at all of us. Wanda and Glenora were smiling at Archibald, I hoped, although some of their smiles went sideways and hit me.

Miss Kramer looked very proud, and Miss Honeychurch was smiling at her dear, dear Shannon.

Shannon was working very hard. He is a better speller than I am, and if I missed I would be glad to see him win. But I had to do my best for the Sixth Grade.

We spelled eight words. Then Shannon got *unbelievable*. The poor guy missed it. He spelled it: *u-n-b-l-e-a-v-a-b-l-e*. He was all mixed up. He had never spelled it that way before, and I knew that he knew better.

I had to spell it right for Miss Kramer and the Sixth Grade.

Then the Sixth Grade had won, but we still had to see who was the winner, Archibald or I.

The next word was *participate*. Archibald spelled it, *p-a-r-t-i-c-a-p-a-t-e*. My ears almost fell off.

"Wrong!" said Miss Remington.

Archibald shook his head and grinned and sat down. His Aunt Grace kept smiling, but I thought she looked very surprised.

Pa and Ma were smiling at me, too, but I knew what I knew.

I took a big gulp of air and spelled it: *p-a-r-t-i-c-c-i-p-a-t-e.*

There was a very loud moan from several people.

"Wrong!" Miss Remington said.

"Trenton J. Conway, Junior," Mom said, "you could spell that word last night."

"That was last night," I said.

Then Wonderful Wanda had to stand up. "He could spell it this morning," she said. "I have this little note to prove it."

She took my note out of her pocket, and it had all those little hearts that she put on it. Was my face red! I did not want everyone to think I am mushy.

Wanda showed it to Miss Remington and said, "Please don't let anyone see it. You know why!"

Miss Remington said, "I think we have a boy, here, who did not want to spell his friend down."

Everyone began to clap.

Well, I am a very honest guy. I knew that Archibald tried to let me win after he was sure the Sixth Grade had won.

I had his note in my pocket with *participate* spelled right. I took it to Miss Remington.

She looked at it and laughed. "What a very fine friendship we have here—two friends who refused to spell each other down!"

My pa spoke up. "I suspect that these heroes were getting hungry and decided to tie it up, which proves that they each have a good nose for banana pie."

So it was a tie, and everyone clapped. They made Shannon stand up, and they clapped for him, too. The prize was a big box of candy which we passed to everyone, and then it was time to eat.

"Well," Wilmer said afterward, "Archibald was a hero again. I suppose Miss Kramer will say we have to let him play and spoil the Bumblebees' chances with the Lawson Lions."

Harley moaned. "I wish good old Ralph had not moved away. Good old Ralph would not have been a hero. He would have been the first guy to be spelled down. Good old Ralph could not spell *cat*, but he could play ball."

"Well," I said, "Archibald thinks he is ready to participate."

"Participate," Wilmer said. "Archibald will come around to your house tomorrow, Trent, and want to bat. You will have to hide out somewhere, or all the Bumblebees will be very mad at you."

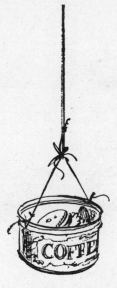

CHAPTER XI

What Happened to Toby

On Saturday morning Ma was cooking, and I was sitting in the kitchen near the doughnuts when I saw something dangle down in the window.

"There is the Lightning Express," I said. "Some beggars have smelled doughnuts."

"Oh, dear!" Ma said. "I don't see how those artists can eat so many doughnuts. Bring it in, Trent."

I pulled the coffee can into the kitchen. A note was in it.

"It's news for me, Kit," I said. "I have to get out of sight, Kit. Give me some of those biscuits and bolt the door tonight, Kit. I'll bed down in the canyon."

Ma gave me three doughnuts in a sack. She said, "You

121

ain't yourself, Blackie. You're afraid. Tell me what you're afraid of, Blackie."

"No time, Kit," I said. "If anyone asks any questions, I ain't been seen in these parts for ten days."

"I'll wait here for you, Blackie," Ma said. "Blackie, do be careful!"

"I'll be back, dead or alive, Kit!" I said.

I hustled upstairs. The note said, "Trent. A. B. sighted."

That meant that Baker was bringing Archibald to pester me to play ball. If I played with him, I knew that Wilmer and Harley and the Bumblebees would be mad.

I hurried to my room and looked out. Sure enough, the long car was in front of the house, and Archibald was getting out of it with a package in his hand.

I went into Hanky and Kymie's room. Hanky and Kymie were both working on the Diesel. "How does it look?" Kymie asked.

"It looks keen," I said. "What are you going to do with the rest of the wall?"

"Ma says we can paint it any color we like," Hanky said. "We like yellow."

"Listen!" I said. Someone was ringing the kitchen doorbell. "It's Brewster," I said. "Men, I am going to hide out. If the slicker ain't out of here by sundown, smuggle me up some rations."

I went in to the twins' room and hid out under Joel's bed. The twins' room is over the kitchen. The clothes chute door in the kitchen was open a little, so I could hear what Archibald said.

He sounded very polite. "Good morning, Mrs. Conway. I came over to—"

"Archibald!" Ma said. "Archibald, that looks—Oh, it couldn't be my bracelet box! But it's so very like it!"

Archibald said, "This is for you, Mrs. Conway. It is the box my watch came in, and it is so much like your bracelet box that I decided to present it to you."

Present it.

Ma said, "Oh, Archibald, you're the kindest boy! But I'm sure you need that box. I can't let you give it to me."

"On my honor," Archibald said, "I have never used this box since the day I got it. Please take it, Mrs. Conway."

I couldn't see, but I guessed that Ma took the box. "It's lovely!" she said. "It's much nicer than the box I had. You are a very thoughtful boy, Archibald, and I thank you. Won't you sit down?"

"Thank you," Archibald said.

I knew he was sitting in a chair that was still warm, because it was the chair where I had been sitting near the doughnuts.

Sure enough, Ma said, "Won't you have a doughnut, Archibald?" I heard a plate being put down on the table, and then I heard a drawer open and close, and I knew that Ma had given Archibald a napkin.

"The doughnuts look very delicious," Archibald said. "Thank you, Mrs. Conway."

Then they began to talk, and it was terrible. Ma didn't care if I starved to death under Joel's bed. Three doughnuts do not last very long, and I began to feel the terrible pangs of hunger as they talked and talked.

Archibald said, "You have a nice house, here, Mrs. Conway."

"Thank you," Ma said. "It is not a very fancy house, but it is a good home for us Conways."

Archibald said, "It is too bad Corky has to visit around."

"Oh, Corky loves it," Ma said. "He can settle down any time he wants to. There is room."

"That is true," Archibald said. "There is room for another bed in every room upstairs. Every room is big enough for three beds."

"Have another doughnut," Ma said.

"Thank you," Archibald said. "They are so delicious that I cannot resist."

Resist.

He said, "I like all the rooms upstairs. I even like the Diesel that Hank and Kymie are painting on the wall. Do you like it, Mrs. Conway?"

"Well," Ma said, "I like it better than some of the other paintings Kymie and Hanky have made. Once they had a cow and a red barn that I was glad to paint out. Before that they made a picture of a family. There were seven children, dressed exactly alike in red shirts and blue pants, standing in a row. The father had a straw hat and a rather horrible beard. The mother, bless her, looked very tired. Don't ask me why, Archibald."

It was quiet for a minute, and I guessed that Archibald was chomping on another doughnut. A fine thing, I thought, a strange boy sitting there in the chair I had warmed, eating all the doughnuts he could reach, while Ma's own boy starved to death and became a lifeless form.

Archibald said, "Hank and Kymie are the same age, but they are not twins are they, Mrs. Conway?"

"No," Ma said. "Kymie's own mother and father died in an accident. Kymie was an orphan when he was only a few weeks old, with no grandparents or even uncles or aunts. His father and Mr. Conway were school friends, and we wanted Kymie to live with us always. We were very happy that we were permitted to keep him."

"Then he is adopted," Archibald said. "For a while, I thought it was Hanky."

Ma laughed. "To tell the truth, Archibald, I don't think their Daddy and I remember, half the time, which one it is. They are just alike to us."

"Well," Archibald said, "there is still room for one or two more boys, if you ever—I mean, if you ever found some boy who would like to live in a house with a Lightning Express and a clothes chute. I mean, if you ever needed one more boy to help clean the basement and mow the yard and bring Corky's teddy bear home— things like that—well, you have enough room. I mean, there might be some boy."

I could hardly hear Ma. She said, "Archibald, dear, would you like another doughnut? And tell me about your dog. His name is Nero, I believe."

"He is gone," Archibald said. "My aunt sent him back to the kennel yesterday. Nero is a one-man dog, and he could not learn to like us. It was not his fault. He is a very fine dog."

I looked at my hands. They looked very thin. I was losing weight fast. I wondered what Ma would say if she came upstairs and found my clothes with a lifeless skeleton in them, a skeleton that used to be Trenton J. Conway, Junior. Then she would have room for another boy, and I hoped she would be happy. My eyes hurt a little, and I winked fast to make them feel better.

Ma went right on talking. She said, "Your mother has been sick a long time, hasn't she, Archibald?"

"I was in Fourth Grade," Archibald said.

"That is a long time," Ma said. "But she is better now, isn't she?"

"It takes a long time," Archibald said.

"But some day she will come home," Ma said. "Won't that be wonderful, Archibald? She will love the big house on Maxwell Street, won't she?"

"I don't know," Archibald said. "We are living in Brookfield now because Aunt Grace thinks there is a lot of fresh air here. But my father is looking for a good town to build another canning factory in when my mother is well. He has been looking a long, long time."

Well, I had been starving a long, long, long time. They were just talking and did not care if I starved to death.

About that time, I fainted dead away. After all, a guy can go without food and water just so long.

But I am happy to report that I did not quite starve to death. After a long time, I heard a voice. It was Shannon's.

"Hey, Trent!" Shannon said. "Are you dead under there?"

"No," I said in a very feeble voice. "I can still wiggle a little."

"Get him, Toby!" Shannon said.

Toby ran under the bed and began to lick my neck and ears. "Cut it!" I said. "Don't you know when a man's almost dead?"

"Wiggle out of there, Trent," Shannon said. "Ma wants you to run to the store for some butter for dinner."

I wiggled out. "Dinner!" I said. "What day is this?"

"Saturday, of course," Shannon said.

"You mean a week from Saturday."

"Come on, wake up!" Shannon said. "You are not Rip Van Winkle. You have only been asleep fifteen minutes. Come on! Archibald is gone. Baker was waiting for him all the time. Archibald came to bring Ma a new bracelet box, and he was only here fifteen minutes."

"Well," I said, "that's what happens when a guy does not have a good watch. He starves in fifteen minutes!"

I went downstairs. Ma was getting dinner, and it was half past eleven, and Shannon was right. It was still Saturday.

"Well," I said, "did you enjoy your lovely visit with Archibald?"

"The poor little boy! I wish his mother would get well soon," Ma said, and she wiped her eyes.

I hurried to the store. I do not like to see Ma cry.

That afternoon I had to mow the lawn, but after supper I met Harley and Wilmer and the guys at the sandlot, and we played ball.

I am sorry to say that we did not do very well. I am a very good batter, but I just was not hitting. The fact is, I struck out.

"The game is going to be a walk-away for Victor Valley and the Lawson Lions if you bat the way you're batting tonight, Trent," Harley said. "You're out."

"O. K.," I said. "Every man has his bad days. Get on the mound, Wilmer."

So Wilmer pitched, and Harley was up to bat. Wilmer pitched wild.

"Ball!" Harley yelled.

"Strike one!" Wilmer said.

I knew how this would end. Harley would chase Wilmer all around the block and by that time it would be so dark we couldn't practice any more.

"Let's go home," I said. "It's getting dark. We can't see the ball. That's what's wrong."

So I went home, and Ma said, "Where were you, Trent? Archibald was looking for you. He had a nice new bat."

"What did he do?" I said.

"Oh, he sat on the front steps and watched for you a while. When I looked again, he was gone. He seemed sad. I believe that boy is worrying about something."

Well, so was I. I was worrying about the big game.

"Skip up to bed, Trent," Ma said. "The boys have had their baths and are all tucked in."

Joel and Jerry and Corky were asleep. Hanky and Kymie and Shannon and I played hide-and-seek until Ma yelled: "Darlings, do you want Daddy to come up there?"

Pa yelled, too. "In this house I want nothing but silence and very little of that!"

It was quiet for a minute. Kymie and Hanky giggled a little.

Then Shannon whispered, "Trent! Where's Toby? Wasn't this his night to sleep with you?"

"I traded with Kymie," I said.

"You sure? I don't think—" Shannon sat up in his bed and kind of hissed. "Kymie! Have you got Toby?"

"No. It's Trent's—hey! We traded!"

Kymie's feet hit the floor. So did mine. We hustled into the twins' room. Joel and Corky were sound asleep in Joel's bed. Jerry was sound asleep, too. Corky had his teddy bear, but Toby was not in sight.

Shannon and Hanky came in. "We'll have to look under the covers," Shannon said.

We pulled the covers down very carefully. No Toby.

"Cover 'em up, and let's get out of here," I said. "If we wake them up, they'll start howling."

We went into my room and looked at each other.

"I wish I was a lawyer like Pa," Shannon said. "When did you witnesses last see the victim alive?"

Kymie began to sniffle.

"Outdoors, right after supper," I said.

"That's when I saw him," Shannon said. "He was playing with a cricket."

"I saw him, too," Hanky said. "That was my last look at him."

Shannon said, "He wasn't in the house tonight. That's queer. He always comes in."

"If he can walk," I said.

"Well, if he got caught somewhere, he would bark," Hanky said.

"If he can bark," I said. "Some cars went pretty fast tonight. Kymie, stop sniffling. You're always giving funerals for things."

"Sure, but they aren't my relatives!" Kymie said. He looked as if he was going to howl. Hank put his arm around him, and he was O.K. until Hank began to sniffle, too.

"Come on, men!" I said. "We'll find the victim. We'll go out the window. Then Ma won't know."

We took off the screen. I hopped out first. I duck-walked over the porch roof and slid down the post. At the bottom two big arms clamped around me, and someone said, "Ha! Got you!"

Somebody screamed bloody murder, and everybody said it was me. If so, I, Trenton J. Conway, have good lungs. I screamed like a siren. Even after I knew it was Pa who caught me, I almost screamed my ears off.

"What's the matter?" Pa said.

"Nothing," I said.

"You aren't eloping with some girl?"

I stopped screaming and looked at him. "A guy who would do that would be crazy," I said.

"I'll remind you of that in nine or ten years," Pa said. "Now shinny up that post and go back to bed. All you other hombres up there, get back to bed!"

So we had to tell him that Toby was lost.

"He is run over by a tanker!" Kymie howled. "A huge, red tanker! He was eaten by a bigger dog!"

Joel and Jerry and Corky woke up and joined the chorus, and nobody ever heard such a noise.

"Louder!" Pa yelled. "I can't hear the sopranos!"

Corky yelled loudest of all. "Toby is losted! Toby is losted!"

Mrs. Miller, next door, stuck her head out the window, listened a minute, and then yelled back into her house. "Pa, have you seen Toby?"

"Toby?" Mr. Miller yelled. "If I see him in my zinnia

bed again, Kymie's going to have a job digging down a little black-and-white——"

"Pa!" Mrs. Miller said. "Pa, you come right out here and help look for Toby."

So Mr. Miller came out and picked up Corky and hugged him. "Hey, hey, hey!" he said. "Stop that squallin'! We'll find Toby. Ma, you call the police!" He took out his handkerchief and wiped Corky's eyes and the teddy bear's eyes and his own. And everybody ran around howling, "Toby! Here, Toby!"

Suddenly a long car stopped in front of the house, and Baker got out of it with something in his arms.

"Toby!" I yelled.

But someone else walked down and took Toby out of Baker's arms. That someone was Ma!

Everyone bunched up around her and hugged Toby and yelled. "Toby! Toby! Welcome home, Toby!"

Baker was still standing there.

"I wish to explain," he said. "Your little dog went home with Archibald by mistake. Archibald seemed to think the dog would be permitted to visit him overnight, but Mrs. Cleveland asked me to drive him home."

"Well," Pa said, "it was an errand of mercy, Baker. I thank you. Mrs. Conway thanks you. Mr. and Mrs. Miller thank you. Oak Street thanks you. If you heard the racket my kids were making——"

"Ha!" said Baker. "Do you call that a racket?"

This was very strange. We all stared at Baker.

133

Baker said, "So you think your kids can bawl! Man, you haven't heard anything yet!"

Then he turned around, walked to the car, started it with a pop, and drove off.

Pa whistled. "Did you hear that, Duchess?" he said to Ma. "That fellow sounded almost human!"

"Poor little Archibald," Ma said.

"Yes," Pa said. "If he didn't have a rich old man of his own——"

"Daddy!" Ma said. "The boys!"

So Pa looked at us. "What are you kids doing out here in your pajamas?" he yelled. "Get back to bed as fast as you can get, and I don't want to hear another peep out of you tonight!"

But Shannon and I whispered a few minutes.

"Our worries about Archibald are over," I said. "He will not ask to play with the Bumblebees. He will be ashamed to speak to us."

"Are you glad?" Shannon said.

I thought almost as long as Wilmer.

"No," I said, "I am not glad. I am sorry for Archibald. He is a rich guy, but he is not happy. He is lonesome. That's why he borrowed Toby."

CHAPTER XII

All in the Game

Well, nobody played on Monday. It was a rainy day.

"A fine thing!" Wilmer said. "The big game is a week from tomorrow. The Lawson Lions will beat us for sure."

"It's raining in Lawson, too," Miss Kramer said. "Don't worry, Wilmer. Not even Victor Valley can play today. Even a major league team would be rained out. Let's forget it and sing. Who has a choice?"

Harley raised his hand. "The Marines' Hymn," he said sadly.

"The Marines' Hymn" did not sound good. It is hard to sing on a rainy day when you are worried.

Archibald was pretty quiet, too. He drummed with his finger a little, and then stopped drumming and looked out the window at the rain. The rest of the guys were just as gloomy as he was.

Then Wanda wanted to sing "Santa Lucia," and none of the boys sang. So Wanda sang louder than ever, and then it was time for arithmetic.

Arithmetic was not so bad. We were learning how to measure things, and the guys were better than the girls.

Just before recess Miss Kramer called Wanda and Glenora and Susie and the girls up to her desk. They whispered and giggled, which is very bad manners.

Then Miss Kramer said, "The girls and I have thought of a nice way to spend recess. Since we have to stay in, and the lower grades are using the gym, the girls will measure the boys for practice. It will be fun to see who is the tallest boy, who has the biggest tummy, and the longest arms, and the biggest chest."

"That's Trent!" Harley said. "Trent's pretty chesty! Haw! Haw!"

"Measure Pitkin's big head," I said, "and you will get a surprise."

This was a joke, and Miss Kramer laughed. Then she said, "I think we will measure every boy's head just for fun!"

We thought she was joking, but she meant it. The girls measured every guy in the room and marked down all the measurements.

Wanda measured me. She kept saying, "Is that too loose, Trent?" and I kept saying, "No, it's too tight." Then she would roll her big blue eyes and look up at me.

When Glenora measured Harely's chest, Harley took a big breath and held it until his face was red. So Wilmer said, "Don't prick him, Glenora, or he will burst with a bang, for sure!"

The girls made pictures of us and wrote the measurements on them.

"I will take them," Miss Kramer said. "They are part of your arithmetic lesson, you know."

Well, it was better than staying in our seats for recess.

Tuesday the rain stopped, but the ground was muddy. We could not play. We stayed on the walk and played catch.

The sun shone, and the wind blew, too; and on Wednesday the ground was dry.

"O.K.!" Wilmer yelled. "No women on the field! Play ball! Trent, you and Harley choose sides."

Well, Archibald was standing there in his good suit, waiting. He had not come to my house since Saturday. He was still ashamed because he had borrowed Toby without asking. I knew he would not ask to play.

I am not a softy, but I am a guy who has feelings; and I felt sorry for Archibald. If I chose sides, I was afraid I might accidentally choose Archibald, and the guys would be mad.

"It's your turn to choose sides, Wilmer," I said.

"I guess you're right," he said.

So he and Harley chose sides, and they did not choose

Archibald. When we began to play, Archibald went over and sat on the walk and watched.

When I was up to bat, there were two men on base. Wilmer was pitching. He called two strikes against me. He pitched again and yelled, "You're out!"

Was I mad! "That was no strike!" I yelled. "Look, Pitkin, you know that was a ball!"

"It was a strike!" Wilmer yelled. "You're just like Ralph! Good old Ralph was always mad, too, when a strike was called on him!"

Right then Archibald stood up. He walked very slowly over to Wilmer and stood in front of him and stuck out his jaw.

"Pitkin," he said, "you are wrong."

My ears almost fell off, I was so surprised. Wilmer stood there with his mouth wide open, and he could not say a word.

All the other guys stood in their tracks and stared, and the girls stopped playing hopscotch and stood around with their eyes wide open. Wanda's eyes looked like two blue saucers.

Archibald was smiling, but it was a tough smile, and he said, "That was no strike, Pitkin. It was a ball, and you know it. And if you don't know it, everyone else does!"

Now this was the truth, and Wilmer knew it. His face was pretty red.

"Hah!" he said. "Look who's talking! Hah!" He threw the ball up about three feet and caught it. Then he dropped it and looked madder than he had before.

"Thanks, Arch," I said. Then I yelled, "O.K.! No women on the field! Play ball!"

Archibald looked at Wilmer. "Remember, Pitkin," he said, "I'll be watching you." He went back to the walk, but he did not sit down. He stood there with his eyes on Wilmer.

Wilmer hitched up his pants and wound up and sent the ball at me. I batted in a home run and brought in two men.

There were no more fights, and my team won.

Thursday it was my turn to choose sides, and the first man I chose was Archibald Brewster. We had two men on base when Archibald came up to bat and Harley struck him out, fair and square.

"A fine thing!" Wilmer said. "With the big game five days away! A fine thing for Victor Valley and the Lions!"

But I clapped Archibald on the back. "It's all in the game, Arch," I said.

"Thanks, Trent," he said. "Very true."

The next time he batted, he got two strikes against him and then batted a homer. Wilmer was right on the job, and Archibald had to sprint fast. He slid home on his good pants, dusted them off, and grinned.

"Not bad, not bad!" Harley said, because after all we are all Bumblebees.

Archibald pitched on Friday after school. Wilmer looked very smart swinging his bat, but he got a surprise.

Archibald could pitch a better curve than any other Bumblebee. He had Wilmer guessing, and when the game was over Harley walked up to him and said, "Arch, my boy, you're O.K. I always said if you had a little time to observe, you would be the best pitcher on the Bumblebee team." He looked at Wilmer. "A-hem!" he said. "I mean second best, of course. Am I right, guys?"

Before the guys could answer, Baker drove up in the long car.

"Well," Archibald said, "I'll have to go, fellows."

He walked very slowly over to the car and talked with Baker a minute. Then he got in and rode away. He did not look back and wave.

"Something is wrong. Maybe his aunt does not want him to play," Harley said. "Baker looked very worried."

"Baker always looks worried," I said.

On Saturday morning I had an invitation from Ma. She invited me upstairs to help her clean my room. I worked very hard, and she talked to me all the time.

She kept saying impolite things such as: "I know what you'll be when you grow up. Take the case off your pillow, Trent. A garbage collector. A boy who keeps orange peels and apple cores and potato chips under his pillow! Trent, if you hit me with that pillow once more . . . . Take it to the porch and bang some of the dust out of it. I hope Mrs. Miller isn't looking! I would like to brag about you to my friends, but what can I say? That

140

your room has the *oddest* smell? Remember, Trent Conway, you are to shampoo your hair before you touch this clean pillow tonight. In fact you come right along to the bathroom now. I am *not* breaking your arm! For once, just once, everything about you is going to be clean. You and your pajamas and your hair and your bed. Honestly, Trent Conway, sometimes your bed looks as if the dog slept in it!"

"Ma, stop jawing," I said. "You will spoil my nerves, and the Bumblebees' captain will need good nerves next Tuesday. Besides, there is soap in my eyes."

"Well," Mom said, "even Corky knows enough to shut his eyes when he has a shampoo."

So I had a bad morning.

In the afternoon I saw Archibald going past our house. He was just walking along.

"Arch!" I yelled. "You want to bat a few?"

"O.K.," he said. "I need some practice."

So he came over. "You have a shampoo?" I said. "Your eyes are red."

"Are they?" Archibald said. He rubbed them. "I have been doing a great deal of reading," he said.

Shannon played with us, and Kymie and Hank. Joel and Jerry ran after the ball.

Archibald could really pitch. I gave him some pointers on batting, but he was not bad at all.

Also he was not happy at all.

At five o'clock Ma called me to the kitchen. "Archibald does not seem happy," she said. "He looks as if he might start crying any time. I am afraid that his mother is worse."

Archibald was sitting on the back porch with his chin on his hands, and Ma looked at him and her eyes were all puddled up with tears.

I hate to see Ma cry. It makes me afraid that I will cry, too, like some baby.

"Kit," I said, "I'd sure hate it if you were sick and away in a hospital."

"I'd hate it, too, Blackie," Ma said.

"I'm sure glad you're right here, cooking and jawing, Kit."

"So am I, Blackie," Ma said. She wiped her eyes. "Go ask Brewster, the Ripper, to take vittles with us."

That night Baker did not come.

Archibald just stayed around and played checkers and watched TV and ate the popcorn Mom popped.

He was very quiet. You would hardly notice he was there.

When Pa began to howl about bedtime, Archibald huddled in his chair and waited.

"Scat!" Pa roared. "Upstairs! You, and you, and you!" He pointed to Corky and Joel and Jerry.

After a while he roared again. "Up those stairs! You and you!"

Hanky and Kymie went up.

In twenty minutes Dad roared again. "Up those stairs! You and you!" He pointed at Shannon and Archibald.

Archibald slipped upstairs behind Shannon. He did not make any noise. He was like a shadow.

Pa was reading again, and Ma was in the dining room. I could hear her at the telephone, talking very low.

In twenty minutes Pa yelled, "Up those stairs! You and . . ." He looked all around. "How come there's only one this time?" he asked. "It always comes out even!"

"Well, you lost count somewhere, Pa," I said.

I went upstairs. Archibald was in my bed.

"O.K.," I said. "But it's my night to sleep with Toby."

"Toby's right here," said Archibald. He flipped back the sheet. Toby was cuddled up in the middle of the bed with his chin on his paws. Arch grinned at me.

I went to bed, and we played hide-and-seek until everyone else went to sleep. Then Archibald and I talked a long time.

Archibald told me why he was not happy.

"My father is coming," he said. "He telephoned my Aunt Grace. She thought I was upstairs. But I was outdoors, and the window was open a little, and I heard her talking. I think that we are going to go away and live somewhere else and wait and wait and wait for my mother to get well, and wait and wait and wait."

"Why can't you wait here?" I asked.

"I don't know," Archibald said. "I don't know what my father said. Maybe my mother is worse."

"Maybe she isn't," I said. "Maybe your father has found a place to build that factory. Why don't you ask your aunt?"

"I am afraid," Archibald said. "She didn't even tell me he phoned, so I am afraid."

Right then Toby squeaked a little. "Hey, hey!" I whispered. "What's the matter, Toby? You want Ma to find out you are up here?"

"I guess I squeezed him too tight," Archibald said.

And then we went to sleep.

CHAPTER XIII

A New Look for Everyone

It seemed that I was asleep for just about two minutes; and then it was morning, and Dad was yanking me out of bed.

He looked at Archibald.

"You can't yank company out of bed," I said.

"Oh, can't I!" Pa said. He yanked Archibald out. Archibald looked very surprised. He had slept in Shannon's striped pajama pants and my spotted top.

"A circus clown!" Pa howled. "Oh, woe! Oh, woe! I never thought one of my kids would end up as a circus clown!"

Corky came in and giggled. "Daddy he is not your kid!"

"Any kid that parks his feet under my table and gets stuck in my clothes chute and sleeps with my dog is my exemption," Pa said.

Then he pulled the covers way down and grabbed Toby by the neck. Toby began to ki-yi as loud as he could.

Ma came to the bottom of the stairs. "Darlings," she said, "I'm coming up there!"

"Off the noise!" Pa said. "And get dressed for breakfast!"

But before breakfast Baker was out in front, and Archibald had to go home.

That took quite a while.

Then we had breakfast.

"What was all the howling about?" Pa said. "Archibald was happy to go, wasn't he?"

"He was *not* happy," I said. "You know he kicked and bawled all the way to the car. His dad is coming today."

"Well, blow me down!" Pa said. He laid down his fork. "Everybody stop sniffling and set me straight," he said. "Do boys kick and bawl nowadays to show their great joy when their dear old dad shows up?"

"That isn't it," I said. "Archibald has to move."

"Does he love his aunt's house so much?"

"No," I said. "He is trying to live with us. But his dad has been looking for a town for his new canning factory. Maybe he has found a town that he likes."

"A fine thing!" Pa said. "Taking my exemption to another town! Men, this calls for action. Stop blubbering and get those flapjacks under your belts. We will storm the fort!"

"I know a short cut," I said. "Take the alley to Caroline Street. Cut kitty-corner to Dennis Place where Wilmer's Aunt Harriet lives. Shinny up her fence and flop down on your stomach and wiggle-waggle across the garage. Then swing into the tree and perch there and whistle for Archibald."

"It sounds fine except for the whistling," Pa said. "I'm afraid I would lose my pucker. How about driving right through the front castle gate at a good forty miles an hour?"

So that was what we did.

Archibald was sitting in the big window having breakfast with his Aunt Grace and his Dad. He was all dressed up in a brand new suit and his watch and ring.

When he saw our station wagon, he jumped up and ran out on the terrace. Toby ran to him and barked, and Archibald picked him up and hugged him.

"Come in!" he yelled. "Come to breakfast!"

"Yes, indeed!" said his aunt. "Will you join us?"

"No thanks," Pa said. "I just came to see about the adoption papers."

"*Adoption papers!*" Archibald's aunt turned white.

"Certainly, Mrs. Cleveland," Pa said. "When I want another boy, I just adopt one. That's how I got one of these fellows. If Archibald is going to eat my flapjacks and soak my soap, I will certainly have to have another exemption for my income tax."

This was a joke, and everyone laughed.

Then Archibald said, "My mother is well! And she's here! She's upstairs, resting from the trip right now! It was a surprise for me!"

Everyone was glad.

"I'm awful glad," I said. "Kit will be awful glad. I mean Ma."

"I'm very happy," Pa said. "And, Brewster, I'd like to talk to you. Our farmers would be glad to raise more peas and corn and beans and beets and cucumbers, if they could sell them here. If there's anything Brookfield needs more than another good pitcher on the Bumblebees' Baseball Team, it is a good canning factory."

"That's what my aunt has been telling me," said Archibald's dad. "Have a cup of coffee, Conway."

They talked awhile, and Mr. Brewster said, "I hoped to find a town where my boy could have a healthy life and some friends. Arch, do you like school here?"

I shook a little. The guys had not been too polite to Archibald for a while.

"Do I like Brookfield School?" Archibald said. "I sure do!"

Was I happy! Was I glad that I had chosen Archibald to be on my team on Thursday!

"This house is much too big," Archibald's dad said. "Mrs. Brewster wants a small one."

"There's a nice little house on Caroline Street," Pa said. He told Mr. Brewster about Ralph's house.

Monday morning Archibald came to school in a plaid shirt, without a tie or ring.

Harley said, "Arch, I almost thought you were good old Ralph!"

When it was time to sing, Archibald raised his hand. He said, "May we sing 'The Marines' Hymn'?"

"As if I didn't know!" Miss Kramer said.

Archibald sang that morning. He sang very loud on one note. He sang just like good old Ralph. When the girls stared, he grinned right back at them.

At recess he made a home run for my team; and when Wilmer struck him out, he was just as mad as Ralph would have been. He chased Wilmer around the schoolyard three times and caught him.

"Pitkin," he said, "since you can't play ball and can't run, do you care to wrestle? If you do, you will not have to be careful of my clothes."

The mailman saved Wilmer from another black eye.

A mail truck stopped in front of the school, and the man yelled: "Fellows! Do you want to give me a lift?"

All the Bumblebees ran to help. There were fourteen boxes, and they were all addressed to the guys, in care of Miss Kramer.

"This one's for you, Arch!" Wilmer said. "I'll carry it for you!" Every fellow had a package. We could hardly wait to open them.

When we got to Miss Kramer's room and saw what was in them, we whooped so loud that Miss Buckmaster and Miss Honeychurch and Miss Remington came running to see.

Every Bumblebee had a baseball uniform and cap!

The uniforms were brown with little gold Bumblebees on the pockets. The caps were gold with a brown letter "B" and a gold and brown bumblebee! Were they keen! Were they neat!

They were from Archibald's Aunt Grace, but Archibald was just as surprised as anyone.

Wilmer hugged Archibald. "Good old Arch! Good old Arch!" he yelled, and Arch hugged him right back.

"Try them on and show us how you look!" Miss Kramer said.

"I hope they fit," Archibald said.

All the girls began to giggle. "Honestly!" Wanda said. She rolled her eyes. "Boys! What do you suppose we measured you for?"

Our ears almost fell off.

"Well," Wilmer said, "this is the first time that girls ever kept a secret!"

So we went to the gym and put on the uniforms and caps and came upstairs. The girls almost fainted with joy.

"Aren't they beautiful?" Wanda said. She was looking right at me. "Oh, aren't they simply cutie-bug?"

"Simply darling!" Glenora said. But she was looking at Harley. His face got kind of red, and he felt of his lip to see if that big black mustache was growing, because pretty soon he will need it to scare Glenora away.

"Honestly," Susie said, "they're simply adorable!"

Adorable!

Miss Kramer said, "I wish I had brought my camera to take a picture while the uniforms are clean."

"Take our picture tomorrow right after the game," Wilmer said. "The uniforms won't be clean, but you will get a picture of the champions. Victor Valley and the Lions can't beat us now!"

151

CHAPTER XIV

Good Old Arch

Victor Valley is a hard man, and he did not intend to lose. Our picnic started at two o'clock; and at two o'clock the bus arrived from Lawson. Victor Valley was the first man off.

His team marched up to the lemonade stand in their blue uniforms, and Victor said, "Lemonade for the Champions, if you please."

Wanda flipped her pony tails back over her shoulders. "Do you mean the Lawson Lion Cubs?" she said in a very sweet voice.

It was funny, and I noticed that Wanda's blue dress and blue hairbows looked almost pretty and made her blue eyes look pretty good, too.

152

"Cubs!" Victor said. "Cubs are baby lions!"

"I know," Wanda said. "They can't even roar. They just mew. Do you want some lemonade for your little lion cubs?"

Then he saw our uniforms. "Ha!" he said. "Very sweet! Well, those uniforms will not win the game."

"We shall see," said Archibald. "Trenton, shall we serve some lemonade to our mothers?"

"Oh, indeed we shall!" Victor said. He grinned. "Conway, how did you ever get such a charming gentleman on your baseball team?"

"It wasn't easy, Victor," I said. "Come on, Archibald."

"Archibald!" Victor said. "What a charming name! If you traded Ralph Jackson for him, you got gypped, Conway."

Archibald only smiled, and we got the lemonade and walked away.

We went over to the chairs where our mothers and Archibald's Aunt Grace were sitting.

Archibald's mother was a very pretty lady, almost as pretty as Ma. She was wearing a pink dress, and she was so happy that she smiled all the time.

"I'll certainly love seeing you win, Trent," she said. "I'll be so proud!"

"Well," I said, "with these keen uniforms, we sure will try!" I felt kind of shaky inside. I hoped we would not disappoint Arch's mom.

The big ball game was the first event. Victor Valley

153

pitched for the Lions. Wilmer Pitkin pitched for us.

In the first inning the Lions scored twice. The Bumble-bees hit two homers and brought in three men, and the score was Bumblebees 5, Lions 2.

"I like to start slow," Victor said.

At the end of the second inning, the score was Bumble-bees 8, Lions 2.

"Ha!" Wilmer said. "Valley, you started so slow that you stopped altogether!"

"I'll show you!" Victor said.

In the third Wilmer struck out two Lions, but the third Lion hit a homer with nobody on base. The next Lion batted the ball right into Harley's hands, and the Lions were out.

Our half of the inning went exactly the same, so we scored one run. The score was Bumblebees 9, Lions 3.

In the fourth, the first Lion batter struck out. Then the Lions loaded the bases, and a fellow named "Freck" drove them in with a homer. Then the score was 9-7. Very close. They tried it again, and the great Victor struck out.

We did not happen to get a run in the fourth, so the score was still Bumblebees 9, Lions 7.

In the fifth inning, the Lions scored twice.

Harley homered, brought in two men, and made a big bow. This made Victor mad. He sent fast balls at the next man and struck him out. The score was Bumblebees 12, Lions 9.

The Lions had two runs in the seventh inning, and we had one. The score was 13-11. They were sneaking up on us.

I hated to admit it, but Wilmer was getting tired. He had not often pitched a full game in practice because someone always got mad at him and chased him around the schoolyard.

I hoped he was not too tired to hold the Lions in the eighth.

But the eighth was not our inning. Three Lions homered, and the third who was named "Sandy" scored two men in front of him.

The next two Lions batted into Harley's hands, and another man was out at first.

The Lions were out, but poor old Wilmer couldn't take the credit. Also, the score was Lions 16, Bumblebees 13.

Victor was sure he would win. He sent them fast. I singled. The next man singled. Pitkin hit a homer and brought us in. Then three Bumblebees struck out and our side was out. The score was 16-16 at the end of the eighth.

So it was all tied up, and the Bumblebees had a talk. I am the captain, and things were pretty desperate. There was only one way to save us, but if it did not work, it would make Wilmer very mad.

I had to take the chance.

"Men!" I said. "Men! Well, men, it's like this!"

"Wait a minute, Trent," Wilmer said. "Men, it's like

this. We've got to win. Arch, here, can pitch a curve that will surprise Victor Valley out of his shoes. Trent, let Arch pitch."

Was that a relief! I thought I was dreaming! Good old Wilmer came through for the Bumblebees.

"A very good idea," I said. I did not say it was my idea.

When Archibald took the mound, I thought Victor would die laughing. But before he could get his breath, Arch struck out two Lions, and Valley did not know why.

He found out. He was the third batter, and Arch's curve ball surprised him so that he was out before he knew what happened.

The game was not over. "Arch held them, but the game is still tied. We've got to score, now," I told the guys. "We don't want any overtime."

Arch came up to bat, and he never had a chance with Valley. Valley struck him out fast.

Wilmer clapped Arch's back. "All in the game, Arch," he said.

The next man up made a base hit. Harley was next. His hit put him on first, and the first batter on second.

I was next. I was scared, too. I knew Valley was mad. He sent me a fast one. I swung and missed. A second fast one. I missed.

I could hear Arch. "Get it, pal. Get it, pal. We've got to win!"

The next one was fast, but I hit it. Zam!

I saw one man get home. Then I saw Harley get home.

I took one last slide, and the next minute I heard Wilmer yelling, "Yea, Conway! Yea, Arch! We won!"

The score was 19-16.

Everyone cheered until my ears ached. I could hear my six brothers yelling loudest of all.

Miss Kramer got some pictures of the champions, and there was only one thing wrong with that. She allowed girls in some of the pictures.

All the Bumblebees' mothers were happy, and Archibald's mother seemed happiest of all.

Wonderful Wanda and Glenora and Susie and the other girls kept choosing us for partners in the games. When we had our picnic lunch, Wanda kept bringing me sandwiches and salad and calling me "Trenty."

Susie forgot she was almost a Seventh Grader and

turned a cartwheel. Then she remembered and blushed and brushed off her skirt and looked at Archibald and giggled. "Hee-hee!"

Glenora brought Harley so much ice cream that he didn't want to come to my house for a few cookies before supper.

He came, though.

When Pa came home, Corky was waiting on the porch. "The Bumblebees winned!" he yelled. "The Bumblebees winned!"

Joel and Jerry screamed from up on the porch. "Pa! Guess what! The Bumblebees won!"

Mr. Miller stuck his head out his door. "Conway," he said, "the Bumblebees won! Yea!" He shut the door.

"No kidding!" Pa said. "That's great!"

Then the Lightning Express came bumpety-bump down from upstairs. "A note for you, Pa!" Kymie yelled.

"Let's see!" Pa said. "The Bumblebees won! Well, well!"

He went into the kitchen. Ma was frosting a cake. Shannon was at the sink scaling a fish. Wilmer and Harley and Archibald and I were sitting at the kitchen table having a few cookies.

"Hi, Pa!" Shannon said, without turning around. "The Bumblebees won!"

"Don't tell me!" Pa looked at the guys and me. "Congratulations! Do you mean the Bumblebees are the champions, without good old Ralph?"

"Ralph?" Wilmer said. "You mean Ralph Jackson? I remember Ralph. He was a great guy. He lived in the house that Arch is going to live in now. He had Archibald's seat at school, too. But Ralph has moved away, and Arch Brewster lives here now."

Harley said, "Arch is just as good a player as Ralph, Mr. Conway."

"That's what I thought," Pa said. He reached into his coat. "Arch," he said, "here's a little token of respect. Don't hug it too hard."

He put something in Arch's hands.

It was a little bit of a puppy—just a little, warm, black and white puppy, with pop eyes.

Arch was so happy that he shook.

His voice shook, too. "He isn't mine, is he?" he said. "I mean, he isn't really mine, is he?"

"He sure is yours, from us," Pa said.

Archibald's eyes got as big as the puppy's. He started to laugh and started to cry.

"Mr. Conway," he said, "I don't know what to say to thank you!"

"Don't say anything," Pa said. "Anything you say may be used against you!"

Archibald started to laugh again, a funny, whispery little laugh. Suddenly he stood up with the puppy in his arms. He went to the door and turned around. "Thank you!" he said. "Thank you!"

Then he turned, ran out the door, pounded down the

steps, and ran away down Oak Street as fast as he could go.

We stood at the windows watching until he turned the corner.

"There goes a good guy," Wilmer said.

"A very good guy," said Harley.

Ma said, "He's going home to make friends with his dog."

"He will be back," I said. "Good old Arch will be back."